Randy & Del

By

N. Fred Botti

© 2018 By N Fred Botti
Printed in the United States of America
ISBN 978-0-9990755-6-2

Special Thanks to
H.L.N.
For his help, support, and understanding.

TABLE OF CONTENTS

CHAPTER 1 – The Move

As the moving van pulled out of the alley, it headed up the road toward Sinclair Boulevard, which would take them back to Interstate 95. It had taken three moving men nearly four hours to unload all of our furniture and boxes. Our new address was 416 Belvedere Road, Dickeyville, Maryland. It was a beautiful, middle class America neighborhood.

I joined my wife, Patti and the kids in the kitchen. Everyone was very busy, unpacking and helping to get the house in shape. Patti had requested a floor plan of the house once we bought it, so she could mark just where every piece of furniture was to go in each room. Since the movers strapped the chest of drawers in place, there was no need to empty them before the move. This was a godsend because once they removed the straps; everything was in place. China, pictures, lamps and loose knick-knacks had to be unpacked. This is what took time, unpacking the many boxes. Then, everything had to be dusted before being placed in its new location.

We moved here from Greenville, Pennsylvania. I had sold real estate there, but when a promotion to office manager in their Maryland office was offered to me, it meant more money. Plus they offered to cover moving expenses! I grabbed it. My wife liked the idea and the kids were young enough to not have any negative feelings about the move. Eddie was eight and Bobby was seven. They would adjust just fine. I had taken a few days off before I reported to Lamont Realty as the new office manager.

Our move was uneventful and Patti had the new house whipped into shape within a few days. To walk into the house, one would never know that we just moved in a week ago. We had enough furnishings to fill all the rooms, so there was very little more for us to buy. Patti's first priority was to get the boys registered into the new school, and that went very smoothly as well. We moved in July and school was scheduled to start after Labor Day. Patti had planned it that way, and she was good at that sort of thing.

The house was in great shape, a Dutch Colonial with four bedrooms and two baths on the second floor. Once inside the front door, you could see how the house was laid out. The foyer led left to the living room, and then into the dining room, which flowed into the large kitchen. There was a powder room, a small laundry area, and a doorway to a spacious two-car garage. A door in the center of the kitchen led to a full sized basement. Next to that doorway was an archway leading to the family room complete with a large red brick fireplace. Another archway led you back to the foyer and front door again.

Our furniture was traditional as well, but eclectic too. Patti had a number of striking oriental pieces including statues and pictures placed just beautifully in the rooms. She had always made our home very cozy and inviting. It was on a one half acre of ground, with beautiful landscaping including several large trees along the sidewalk. In front of the house were several small leaved oak and maple trees that turned the most unusual shade of orange and beige with red streaks running through them when the weather got cooler. There were also some sugar maple trees out in front, with breath taking shades of gold in the fall. The only thing that we did before we moved in was to have the rooms painted. My real estate connections helped with getting a good deal on the painting contract.

About four blocks up the road and just off of Sinclair Boulevard on Dora Lane was a strip mall shopping center. It consisted of a variety of stores including a drug store on one corner; then a liquor store, sporting goods store, barber shop, hardware store, and dollar store. A large supermarket was at the other end, with a bank annex and ATM next to it. In back of the stores was an alley, which led to two more businesses, built into the basement of the stores from around the front. Here you would find a beauty shop, in the basement of the sporting goods store, and the *Angie's Lounge*, located in the basement of the barber shop, and the sporting goods store.

The *Lounge* was a unique little place serving drinks and lite fare including pizza, homemade hot soups, a variety of deli sandwiches, and fresh-cut French fries. The locals referred to it as just, *The Lounge*. It's a pretty good business too; opened at 11:00 am and closed at 2:00 am. It is owned and operated by Tony and Angie Seric. There was always someone there, individuals and groups, but mainly residents of the area. The décor was interesting too, a collection of sofas and large tables. Large overstuffed chairs and small dining room style chairs were scattered around the space. The Lounge occupied the entire basement of the barber shop with the exception of a kitchen and bar at the back.

Across the street on Dora Lane was a huge Catholic Church and school complex. The Holy Cross Church included a large rectory housing five priests, a convent for seven nuns, employed a number of lay teachers, and had an elementary and high school. There was a large auditorium too, with plenty of parking. There was always something going on at the church or the auditorium in the evenings, so there were always people coming and going. This was our new neighborhood.

CHAPTER 2 – The Neighborhood Cookout

A fter a few weeks in the neighborhood, we had pretty much settled in and were getting acquainted with the area. The Lamont Realty Offices were located in the Hamilton Valley Business complex, not too far from where we lived. The office was clean, spacious, and on the ground floor of an exclusive area. I made a few changes with workflow and postings. I had some other changes to make, but those could wait for a while. I didn't want to change too much at once. There were eight full-time and four part-time sales persons in the office, plus three clerics. The senior salesperson was a gal named Lynne who is in charge when I am not there. I liked everything about my new job, especially because it was so close to home.

During my third week on the job, I received a phone call from my wife Patti. Her message was short and sweet.

"Don't dilly dally after work, come straight home. The neighbors are giving us a *Welcome to the Block Cookout* tonight."

"Should I pick up anything?" I asked.

"No, the neighbors have furnished everything," she replied.

I rushed right home, changed into some comfortable clothes and joined the party. I had met my next-door neighbor Randy Bishop, his wife Debbie, and their two children Josh and Linda before. They were very close in age to my two boys, Eddie and Bob. Randy is twenty eight and his wife is twenty six. Patti and I are the same age, twenty seven. So you can see that this is a pretty young neighborhood. We met the other residents - members of our road - eight in total. The Fayes, the Mitchells, the Rogers, and the Nichols. The Mitchells, Rogers and Nichols all had children too, and the kids seemed to be getting acquainted and having lots of fun. Patti and I introduced us as Chris and Patti Delinar, from Greenville, Pennsylvania noting that the town was about thirty miles outside of Pittsburgh. We spent the entire evening getting acquainted with our new neighbors. In the course of the evening, it came out that no one ever called me Chris, but rather "Del" from my last name Delinar. So from then on in, I was called "Del."

The cookout was a complete surprise to Patti and me. Randy knew about it, but was sworn to secrecy by Debbie. There was plenty of food, something for everyone; chicken breasts, hamburgers, hot dogs, grilled veggies, plus all kinds of salads. For dessert, there was ice cream and cake. We then learned that all of their kids went to the Catholic school just up the road. The school had a comprehensive athletic program that was outstanding. My kids and Randy's kids were tickled to death to be there. The boys were interested in basketball. Linda was interested in the skating program. My oldest son Eddie did some ice skating, but never showed an interest in pursuing it. He'd rather play basketball. Seems like they all found their niche.

Randy and I had become acquainted the day we moved in, and have become friendlier since then. Patti and Debbie also connected and were becoming close friends. Neither one worked outside of the home. The more time they spent together, the more they seemed to have things in common. Debbie was an antique collector, and her home was furnished with exquisite Early American pieces. Patti would accompany Debbie when she went hunting for a picture or some piece of Early American furniture. Debbie was becoming pretty sharp at recognizing nice antiques. Patti, on the other hand, was an avid collector of anything that looked expensive, and usually was. She furnished our home with whatever she liked. It was eclectic, but her taste was impeccable. She had a real knack for putting objects of furniture together that looked professionally placed.

When everyone else had gone home after the party, I helped Randy clean up. Since we were neighbors, we used both backyards. Our yards adjoined each other without a fence or rail to separate them. We actually had the benefit of both yards and it made our yards look twice as big. The gals were putting salads away and would join us later for a drink.

With everything done, Randy and I sat outside on the patio enjoying a drink. I took a good look at Randy and decided that this man was *very* handsome. He was six foot tall, slender, with dishwater blonde hair - as my mother used to say. He had very little fat on his frame, if any. He appeared to be in excellent shape. Randy was always on the go, so he had little time to gain any weight.

Randy worked with his father at the local hardware store, *Bishop's Hardware*. His dad owned the store, and according to Randy, it was pretty busy too, there was always someone coming in to buy something. His dad had helped me the few times I went in to get needed items for the house. Randy introduced me to his dad, *Big Ed*. Big Ed and I hit it off right from the start. He would tease and cut up with me when there were no customers in the store. He soon began to refer to me as his *second son*.

Big Ed had been a Bay Pilot on the Baltimore Harbor. Bay Pilots get paid a hefty salary - six figures and up - to start. There are many that want these jobs, but they are highly selective. You must be recommended by a Bay Pilot in order to even get into the training program.

(Editor's note) Bay Pilot is a nautical term that has its roots in ancient Phoenician maritime history. The pilot is the chief person duly qualified to steer ships into or out of a harbor or through certain difficult waters. His familiarity with the water he is traversing allows the ship to be safely navigated to its port. Pilots are in command of large ocean-going commercial ships such as tankers, passenger, container and general cargo ships.

Ed had also made some good real estate investments. He bought nearly sixty acres of land when it was dirt-cheap. Today, Hamilton Valley is very near the property he bought. He and his wife, who passed away about eight or nine years ago, built a large, field stone home on their property. When his wife died, he and Randy lived there until Randy got married and moved out.

Sometime later, Big Ed suffered a stroke. While recovering from that, he had a heart attack and required by-pass surgery. While Big Ed was mending, he and Randy had a serious discussion. As a result, Big Ed would sell off all his property and retire, so to speak. He found a condo about two blocks from Randy, paid cash for it too. Big Ed wanted to be close to Randy and Debbie, just in case anything else was to happen. He also put the condo and all its contents in Randy's name, so that Randy could avoid paying taxes on this property when he passed. You could safely say that Big Ed – Edward Bishop - was a millionaire.

After being confined to his condo for a few months, Big Ed got a good case of cabin fever. He wasn't used to staying home all day, so he went out shopping for something to buy that would keep him busy. He found several business opportunities but didn't care for either the location or the price. So he kept looking until one day, while he was visiting Randy, he stopped in the hardware store at the strip mall. He overheard the owner talking to a real estate salesman. He was talking about selling the hardware store and wanted to put it on the market that weekend. Well, that was all Big Ed had to hear! He approached the owner and salesman and introduced himself. The three of them had a pleasant conversation and Big Ed had liked everything he heard, except for the price.

After a little negotiating, the owner was willing to lower the price, especially when Ed offered to pay cash and not finance the deal through the bank. It was agreed that he could take possession of the store and its contents in two weeks. The only stipulation made was that Big Ed had to agree to keep the current staff and not let them go. Two middle-aged women worked at the store, Gladys and Hazel, along with a young man, Tony, who was a college student. Big Ed easily agreed.

Big Ed then went over to see Randy and tell him the good news. The strip mall was only two blocks from his condo and just about four blocks from Randy's house. He also had the idea to ask Randy to help him run the store. Randy would have to quit his current manager's job with the insurance company, but his father offered to pay him much more money than he would have made if he stayed. After all, Randy was designated the sole beneficiary of everything his father owned. Randy agreed without hesitation.

Things at the cookout began to wind down, and clean-up had started.

"Randy, can I help you put anything else away?" I asked.

"Nope, I'm almost done," answered Randy, "Sit there and enjoy your drink. I'll join you in about two minutes. Thanks for the offer anyway."

Sure enough, he was back in a few minutes. He refreshed my drink, made himself one, pulled a chair closer to me, and then sat down.

"Did you have a good time tonight?" he asked.

"I did," I replied, "And whom do I have to thank for this cookout?"

"Debbie had her hand into this up to her elbow," said Randy and then he began talking about some of the neighbors.

"The Fayes are very aloof, not too sociable as well, but we seldom see them. They spend most of their time out of town. Your next-door neighbors, Wayne and Lenore Rodgers, travel a lot, too. When they're home, they're friendly, but they're seldom home. I'm even surprised the Fayes and the Rogers made it tonight. The rest of the folks, the Mitchells and the Nichols, are friendly, but to a point. If you see or speak to them in passing, its fine, but Debbie and I got the distinct message that they just don't want to get too friendly."

"Thanks for bringing me up to date with the folks on the block. A little background is good to know."

I took a good long look at Randy and had to tell him,

"Randy, *you* are a very handsome man. I've been looking at your face, your profile. You could easily get a part-time job as a model. I'm surprised someone hasn't said something to you before now."

"Well, thank you, Del," he said, squeezing my knee. "That was so nice of you to say. Not to brag or anything, but I've been told that before. You know, when I was in college, a good friend of mine, Joel, had the looks that people would die for. He was recruited by an agency for a modeling job, and he took it. He felt that I was handsome enough to get a job there too, but I refused. Our paths didn't cross again for about three or four years. But when we met again, we decided to have lunch. I wanted to talk to him about how his career was going."

"Are you still modeling?" I asked Joel.

"Yes, I am."

"You look great, that career must be treating you well."

"Bullshit," he replied, "You don't want to hear what I have had to do to be called an active model. Men and women, mainly young girls, usually become sex toys to some of the most powerful people in the industry."

"Meaning men taking advantage of the younger girls?" I asked.

"Hell yes, but the young men are taken advantage of too. There are some who want the male models to have sex with them or they can just look for a new career. I've learned that the bigger the cock, the better your job is. Some models do make it on their own, but if you're not one of them, stay away. It can be a lousy life. One false word against you from a higher up, and you're done; whether you've done anything wrong or not. Young people know this but yet they still flood the market and modeling agencies hoping to be discovered and make it big."

"Well, why don't you quit? You have a college degree. You don't need that kind of life."

Joel laughed at me and said, "Are you kidding? It's the glamour, the prestige, and of course the money is fabulous! The girls go for designer clothing, jewelry, expensive cars, and sugar daddies. *Me?* I just want the money. Where would I ever make that kind of money posing for an after shave lotion, cologne, or shirt and necktie ads for men?"

"And he's still modeling," said Randy. "I've seen his pictures advertising after shave, cologne, and sportswear, in several magazines."

"But, how about you Del, you're handsome and slender enough to be a model. What's holding you back?"

"Not me, I like being a family man with my wife and kids. I enjoy a job where I'm my own boss. Modeling is not for me."

Randy laughed and said, "Well, that's two of us who are happy with what we have." He mixed us another drink and we began getting better acquainted. A bit later Patti and Debbie joined us for a nightcap. After we had our drinks, we called it a night and went our separate ways.

CHAPTER 3 - The Picnic at Edgewater Dam

As time passed, the Bishop and Delinar families became quite close. A few weeks after the cookout, Randy planned a picnic for us at Edgewater Dam, located about five or six miles from our homes. The drive to the dam was quite scenic. When you entered the driveway to the dam, there was a huge restaurant where you could get hot food, bottled water, soda, coffee and live bait for fishing. There were countless picnic areas with tables and benches, some having charcoal grills as well. Further on, there were four large ponds that fed into the lake where you could rent a boat, fish from a dock, or swim in the protected areas. There were countless trails for schools to use for biology and science class field trips too. Randy pulled me aside and pointed to some not-so-traveled paths.

"I hear that these are lover's lanes at night, no lights of course. But, I also hear that there's plenty of other activity after dark as well," he laughed.

The kids had a ball at this place. There was plenty to see and do. A doe and her two fawns were grazing near our picnic table. They seemed not to be afraid of humans. Then the kids soon found out they could go swimming in the roped area of the dam since the lifeguards were on duty now. Randy cooked hamburgers and hotdogs and we had us quite a picnic.

After we ate, we sat around on some chairs that Randy had brought from the hardware store. We sipped our soft drinks, and just became very lazy and relaxed. Suddenly, the kids were squealing. They really sounded excited. Randy and I went over to see what was causing such a commotion. We found that they had a little snake cornered at the trunk of a tree. They were using sticks and twigs to torment the poor creature.

Randy cautioned them, "You have a baby snake cornered, but just remember, he's a baby, and somewhere nearby his mother is going to look for him and when she finds him, she'll find you hurting her baby. What do think will happen then? She'll go after you!"

They threw the sticks down and ran back to the table.

"Are we safe now? Will she come after us here?"

"No" said Randy, "The baby wasn't hurt and the mother didn't see what you were doing."

"Is that true?" whispered Patti, who is deathly afraid of snakes.

He winked in reply, and Patti and Debbie began to snicker. The kids didn't stray too far from the table after that. When it was time to leave the dam we stopped at the restaurant to have some ice cream sundaes. No one said no to that.

CHAPTER 4 – The Broken Window

The old saying time flies rings true. A year has gone by, and we've all adjusted well to the new house, the new neighborhood, the children's new Catholic School, and my new job at Lamont Realty. Randy was right about the other neighbors on our block. We seldom saw them, and if and when we did, it was a hand wave "hi," and that was it. They were a very different bunch, to say the least.

It was September, and fall was just beginning to open her beautiful wardrobe of colors. Mother Nature was putting on an incredible show. Sugar maple trees were a beautiful shade of gold, while the red, rust, and orange leaves of the others complimented the varieties of evergreens. It truly was a wonderful site.

It wasn't busy at the hardware store, so Big Ed sent Randy home. He told him that if it got too busy, he would call on his cell to have him come back. Lamont Realty wasn't too busy either, so I left early - a manager's prerogative. Randy was home when I pulled into the driveway.

The kids were playing ball in front of the house, so the two big kids, Randy and I, had to join them too. After a short time, one of the kids missed the ball and it crashed into my clubroom cellar window. When Randy and I looked at the damage, we realized it was only the storm window that was broken. The inside window was not damaged at all. Randy said that he could get a piece of glass from the hardware store and we could fix it in about half an hour. Patti, Debbie, and Linda had gone to a fashion show and dinner at the church, so they wouldn't be home until after 8:00 pm. Thank God! We wouldn't have to get lectured about playing ball around the house. I would make it a point to tell the kids to keep mum about the broken window.

Randy returned with the glass for the window. I told the kids to go up to the den and play a game or watch television. They decided to watch one of their favorite shows and hurried up the stairs. Randy and I moved the end table and lamp out of the way, and put two folding chairs beneath the broken window. All we had to do was remove the damaged glass, insert the new piece, tighten the screws, and then lock it into place. After the broken glass was cleaned up, Randy asked me to hold the inside window up so he could lock in the storm window. We were standing on the folding chairs, working side by side. I was holding the curtain rod up so Randy could finish the job, but I had to stretch over his head to put it back into place. Our legs were pressing against each other, then as I went to step back; I turned my head and came face to face with Randy.

Our eyes met and neither of us moved. His eyes were intriguing, the sexist I'd ever seen. We focused intently on each other. Before I knew what was happening, Randy reached his hand behind my head and gently pulled me closer to him. Then he kissed me on the lips, ever so gently. I raised my arms and hands to push him away, but instead my hands slid over his shoulders. I put my arms around his neck to continue the kiss. My heart was beating rapidly and I seemed to be having anxiety pains as well.

"Christ, what's happening here?" I thought. "Shouldn't I be pissed and mad as hell?"

"Del, what just happened here?" Randy asked in a husky voice. "I'm really so . . ."

"Stop," I said.

"I don't know what happened here but don't apologize, I really enjoyed it," I quickly answered. "You see I still have my arms around you."

"So you do," Randy answered.

Then Randy kissed me again and this time it was not too gentle. His tongue darted around my lips until he entered my mouth and explored every inch of my mouth. Not to be out done, I did the same thing to him. While all this was going on, I felt a slow growth in my groin area. I was getting an erection. Just then the chair slipped and we both fell backwards onto the sofa. We laughed wildly.

"Are you okay?" Randy whispered huskily.

"Yes," I answered in that same husky tone of voice. I realized then that he had fallen on top on me. I could feel his erection too.

"I don't know about you Randy, but I need a drink."

He agreed. So I went to the bar and made two scotch and waters for both of us. When I sat down on the sofa, he put his arms around me and I got another kiss. Then he took my hand and guided it down to his zipper. He still had a hard on, and he placed my hand on it. My heart started to beat faster and the whim-whams in my stomach wouldn't stop. Then I felt his hand on my cock, which was hard and red hot, and he groped me several more times.

"Randy, stop!" I said.

"What's wrong?" he asked surprisingly.

"You got me so hot, that if you don't stop squeezing my cock, I will shoot," I answered.

"Is that all?" He reached over to the chair to pick up the cloth he had used to wipe the new window glass.

He pulled down my zipper, grabbed my cock and said,

"I can see you didn't get cheated."

After three or four gentle jerks, I exploded into the cloth he provided. He then pulled his zipper down, and put my hand on his hard cock.

"I can see you're well-endowed too," I whispered.

He shot faster than I did. After we cleaned ourselves up, I put the cloth in a paper bag threw it into the trash. We were soon kissing again.

"The kids!" I suddenly realized. "Let me check on them."

I ran up the stairs only to find them in the den watching a video and eating pretzels and potato chips. I came back down to the sofa, turned on the television for background noise, and turned to talk to Randy.

"Randy," I said, "I don't know what happened. I'm not gay. I love my wife, my children, and my life as a family man. I hope this doesn't label me now as *gay*."

"I'm not gay either," Randy replied. "I share the same values as you. I don't want anything to interfere with my current family lifestyle. It goes without saying that I am very fond of you, Patti, and the kids. You're like my own family."

Losing some of the hoarseness in my voice I replied,

"I feel the same way about you and your family, but I really enjoyed what happened between us today. I hope we don't have to lose it."

Randy grinned and asked,

"Is what just happened going to put a damper on our friendship, Del?"

"I certainly hope not, Randy. This is something that just happened. It wasn't planned, was it?"

"Hell no," replied Randy, "I happened to turn around and see your face so close to mine, I just got an impulse that I couldn't resist. You looked so beautiful and innocent, I had to kiss you, it may happen again. Would you be offended if it did?"

"No, I don't think so. I'm sorry if I seem awkward but I have never had sex with a man before."

"You have never had a blowjob?" asked Randy.

"Oh yes, in college there were a few guys who let it be known that they were available for blow jobs, but they were my age, not grown men. Have you ever had sex with a man before?"

"After tonight I won't be able to say no," Randy replied.

"Randy, whatever we do, we have got to be careful. I don't want anything to jeopardize our families." With that, we were embraced in another long passionate kiss.

"Del, when I see you, I want to hold you, kiss you. I can't get enough of you."

"When you walk in a room Randy, my heart beats faster and I think there are flamingos flapping around in my stomach!"

"You too?" asked Randy, "Flamingos are in my stomach too, but I think they're wearing combat boots." We both laughed and continued to sip our drinks.

"I have never kissed a man on the lips before," I said. "There is something sensuous and exciting, almost fascinating about it. It was interesting and I have such a warm feeling about it."

"I don't know how to explain it either, but I did enjoy it," replied Randy.

We sat and talked about our likes and dislikes. It was amazing how much we had in common. It's really such a small world. We had two more scotch and waters when the girls came home from the church fashion show and dinner. The kids couldn't wait to tell them about the broken window. With that, I realized I had forgotten to tell them to keep quiet about it. Patti went over to survey the damage but found none. Randy and I explained what had happened, and of course, got our lecture about playing ball in front of the houses.

"Use the alley next time boys," Patti said sternly. "Hey, what did you all have for dinner?" she asked.

"DINNER!" We both exclaimed. "We completely forgot about *dinner*," I answered.

"What about the boys, Del? Didn't you think to feed them?" Patti snapped.

Eddie, my son, chimed in, "Oh Mom, don't worry. We had pretzels and potato chips, chocolate chip cookies and soda."

I explained that in getting the window repaired, we had forgotten about dinner. Randy suggested that we order some pizzas to make up for that, adding that he'd go pick them up if I'd ride along. Everyone agreed it was a good idea.

Thirty minutes later, we were all seated in the den, eating pizzas, including the gals. Even though they had been at the church fashion show and dinner, they couldn't resist at least one slice of pizza. Debbie confessed that she had spent about three hundred dollars on clothes for herself and Linda, mainly. She also bought something for her mother. Patti said that she spent about two hundred fifty dollars on herself and more money on a few things for her mom. After a while, we sent our kids to bed. The adults all had a nightcap, and then Randy took his brood home. Patti and I called it a night too. I had a hard time falling asleep though, I was reliving the earlier events of the evening, and wondering how Randy was doing.

The next morning while backing out from my garage, I saw Randy getting the newspaper from his lawn. He waved for me to stop. My heart did a flip-flop again, and the flamingos were working on my stomach. I pulled to the curb and he walked to the car.

"How are you doing, Del?"

"Pretty good," I replied.

"No guilt trip as a result of last night?" Randy asked.

"No," I replied, "Although, I had a hard time falling asleep."

"I didn't have any guilt trip either," replied Randy. "We shouldn't have any. We are both responsible people, provide for our wives and children. We both live in nice homes. Our families are not neglected. What happened last night has no bearing on our feelings for them at all."

Randy was leaning on the driver's car door gently sliding his hand on to my arm giving me an affectionate squeeze.

"We will be just fine. Call me on my cell if you should leave the office early today."

"Okay, I'll plan on it," I answered.

As I drove away looking at him in my side mirror, my heart skipped a beat or two. Then those damn flamingos started working on my stomach again. I can't explain it; just the sight of him affects me that way.

The office at Lamont Realty was doing just fine. Several new listings had come in from people who had given up on trying to sell their homes on their own. Business for us, that was good. By 2:00 pm I was ready to call it a day. I remembered Randy wanted me to call him, which I did. He told me the day was pretty slow and his dad was going to close early, so Randy could leave early too.

"Meet me at The Lounge, Del."

I agreed, and as I walked into The Lounge about twenty five minutes later, I saw that Randy was seated at a corner couch with two scotch and waters on the cocktail table. We shook hands cordially and I sat next to him taking a sip of my drink.

The Lounge was practically empty. Two men were seated near the bar; one was obviously a salesman trying to close a sale for storm windows. Randy inquired how things were at the office, and I told him that I could have stayed home for all that happened today. My office staff is good and they do a good job. Just then, I noticed that Randy's thigh and leg were brushing against mine. Every so often he would flex his leg, which began to stimulate my leg and thigh. I returned the favor. While we were sipping our drinks, we were having intercourse with our legs. No one could see what was going on and Randy and I engaged in some shoptalk while we sat there. Several more men came into the lounge. One of them was an attractive young man about thirty something.

"Hi Randy," he said as he crossed over to our sofa.

Randy stood and introduced him to me, "This is Andy, and he's the hair stylist at the barbershop next door to the hardware store. He does my dad's hair and mine too."

Andy was casually dressed but his hair was attractively styled, a real eye catcher. Randy invited him to join us and he did. After a few minutes of conversation, I detected a faint feminine accent and flair normally associated with gay people.

"I work next door to Randy and his father. I'm part owner of the barber shop and I also cut hair as well as style it." As he was talking, he was eyeing my hair. "I'd love to style your hair if you would let me."

"I'll give it some thought next time I need a haircut," I replied.

Andy explained that he is often called Dee. His nephew couldn't pronounce Andy when he was small but he always called Andy - *Dee* - and it stuck with the family. To this day, some of the family still call him Dee. We finished our drinks and Randy said that we had to leave. As I got up to leave, Andy felt my head.

"You have a healthy head of hair," he said, "I'd really like to style your hair. Here's my card, give me a call and I'll set up an appointment for you. You'll be amazed how much a good hair style can change your appearance."

I took the card and thanked him as Randy and I left.

"You should let him style your hair, he does mine," said Randy.

"Your hair always looks great" I replied; "maybe I will let him do it."

"You know that he is gay, don't you?" said Randy.

"I saw some feminine traits but I just met him today, so no, I didn't know he was gay."

Randy added. "It's no secret, he doesn't deny it, but he doesn't advertise it either. He's a pretty good guy. Most people around here like him."

Randy checked again with Big Ed. Business was still slow and he was closing early, so Randy could go home. Since Randy walked to work and I drove, he rode home with me.

CHAPTER 5 – New Opportunities

"Are you and Patti going to be home tonight?" asked Randy.

"As far as I know, we'll be."

"Well then, I'll be over after dinner to talk to you," he replied.

"About what?" I asked.

"Wait and see nosy," Randy responded.

"Thanks for the ride, I'll see you later."

I was very curious about why Randy wanted to talk to both Patti and me. I mentioned it to Patti during dinner and she didn't have a clue. Debbie hadn't said anything to her either. Around 7:30 pm, Randy came in and said Debbie would be over later.

"The reason for my being here tonight is to offer Del a job, that is, if he wants it. My dad may look great for his age, he's slim and handsome, but his health doesn't match his appearance. There is so much that he cannot do. The stairs and the stepladder do him in when we are busy. And, he's bullheaded. He'll do things that he isn't supposed to do rather than ask for help. When I catch him doing these sorts of things, I give him hell, but it's like talking to a brick wall. With the holiday season coming, he will need some additional help," Randy explained.

"I didn't realize the situation," I replied.

Randy paused for a moment, and then continued, "When dad bought the store, there was an old man named Petey who offered to work and help out when he could do it.

He had worked for the previous owner and wanted to help out. Petey was not part of the deal that dad made with the previous owner about keeping his help - the two ladies and a college student. There was no obligation to keep him. Dad sees him once or twice a week, if that often. Petey doesn't have a schedule; he just shows up when he feels like it, but he is helpful when he's there. My dad suggested you, Del. He knows that he can trust you and you could help out during the busy season on Saturdays and Sundays. He plans to extend the store hours and the evening hours as well. If you could do it without interfering with your full time job. Petey might show up and be of some help too."

"It won't interfere with me, said Patti as she finished up making ice tea for the kids and us. "I have all my work done before Del gets home from work; his evenings are free. It might pose a problem on weekends, but I can't really think of any right now."

"Sorry I'm late. I'll have some ice tea too," said Debbie as she came in the door.

Randy brought her up to date on what had been shared.

"Good choice. Are you interested?" asked Debbie.

"Yes, I am," I replied, "but how soon do you have to know?"

My heart was racing and the flamingos were having a foot race in my stomach. Imagine being with him on the weekends. My mind was shouting, "YES!" But, I didn't want the wives to think I was too eager for this chance. I wanted them to think I had to figure out my work schedule and what I might have to give up by working at the hardware store.

So instead I calmly said, "Let me check a few things at the office and I'll let you know in a day or two. Is that okay with you Randy?"

"That's great Del," said Randy; "at least I know that you're considering it."

True to my word, I told Randy two days later that I could help him out during the holidays.

"I'd be disappointed if you would have said no, very disappointed," giving me a warm handshake. I returned his handshake with a tight grip… he got the message.

"Del, any time you have some free time from here on in, come into the store and get familiar with the layout, merchandise, and basement stock. I'll put you on payroll. You're officially a member of the staff and I'll get you set of keys. I'm usually there all day. Have you told Patti?"

"Yes, during breakfast this morning. She's cool with it," I replied.

CHAPTER 6 - A New Plan

I finally broke down and let Andy style my hair; I needed a haircut anyway. But believe me, there is a big difference between a haircut and hair styling. After this, I made up my mind that I'll never get another haircut; it's hair styling for me. Haircuts run less than twenty dollars, while hairstyling can run twenty five or more, but well worth the difference. Andy explained that he looks at the neighborhood and prices his services accordingly.

After I left the barbershop, I went to the hardware store and spent some time getting acquainted with the merchandise and their method of record keeping. Working alongside Randy did not stop my heartbeats, flip-flops or the flamingos from their ritual dance. Just being near him gave me those feelings. I wanted to grab him, hug him and smother him with kisses, but instead, I had to remember my place and refrain from such an outburst.

After the shop closed, we went down to The Lounge for a drink and there was Andy sitting alone. He waved to us, and then came over to join us on the sofas.

"Like your hair?" he quipped.

"Yes I do," I replied. "You know I'll be back."

"I hope so. I never lose a customer," said Andy. "You're soon due too, Randy. Make an appointment and I'll take care of you before the rush," he added.

"Will do!" replied Randy.

We ordered drinks and discussed the rapidly approaching holiday season. Andy was glad to learn that I would be helping Big Ed.

"Things are looking up on our little strip mall. Any plans for the holidays, or is it too soon?" asked Andy.

We both replied that it was too early, but we would start soon.

"Well, it won't be long before they start putting up those damn god awful Christmas decorations. And we pay for that shit," complained Andy. "They should get a couple of gay guys to decorate. They'd put this place on the map. You'd have people coming here from all over just to see the decorations."

"Why can't we do it? Is it a closed deal?" I inquired.

"Well," Randy added, "I think we would have to contact all the shop owners on this strip, and see how they feel about it. If they're all are in agreement, we then must approach the management of this strip and see what they say. They have the final say so."

"And if they say yes," said Randy, "we need to get some gay guys who could do this."

"I'll get them, don't worry about that," replied Andy. "And, it might be cheaper than what we pay now."

"Looks like we have a project on our hands guys," said Randy, a few days later. "I contacted the reality firm who does our strip decorating and they have no problem if we want to decorate instead of them. Now that we have their approval, we can contact the store owners or managers."

Andy decided that just the three of us could canvas the owners on the strip, the less people involved the better. We would find out what they contributed, and then decide what we could do instead. We agreed to start talking to the shop owners on Saturday morning, and then to pool our findings at a meeting in The Lounge that night when we were finished. We left with a feeling that something had been accomplished.

Saturday morning found us going to each store and talking to the store owners or managers. We met at The Lounge around lunchtime, loaded with information. After ordering some food and drinks, we discussed our findings. It seemed that each storeowner paid about one hundred dollars for decorations, while the drug store and the food market paid more because their stores were bigger. Almost all of them were eager for a change. They were tired of the same old green garland inter-twined with colored lights, wreath on the door, lights around the roof top, and artificial snow on the windows. The big expense, they had been told, was the cost of labor. We also found out that The Lounge and the beauty shop put up their own wreath and lights and were not part of the main strip upstairs. They pay their own way.

We decided that Andy would make some contacts for supplies and workers, which he was most eager to do. We had agreed on the weekend before Thanksgiving to start decorating. We also agreed on the same price that the owners had already been paying, and everyone was in agreement that is was do-able.

On Monday morning, Andy had told Randy that he had four guys willing to help with the Christmas decorations. They were going to come out and look at the shopping center first. Then they'd meet to decide on how to make it look most attractive. They get the funds from us, buy what they needed, and begin to decorate the weekend before Thanksgiving. Randy called me and relayed all the information.

"Sounds like we have a pretty good deal going," I said to Randy.

He agreed and wanted to know if I would be leaving early today. I answered that I'd love to but I had to wait and see what the new people were doing.

"Call me if you do and I'll meet you at The Lounge," replied Randy.

It was no surprise to Randy or me, that I meet him in The Lounge around 3:30 pm for our usual drink. Randy said that his father had talked to him about attending some craft shows that were coming up before the holidays, but Big Ed didn't feel up to it. He wanted to know if Randy and I would go instead and do some buying for the shop. Randy added that all expenses would be paid by the business. There were three craft shows coming up soon. The first one would be in Washington, DC, a three day show - Friday, Saturday and Sunday.

"Dad said that since you're on payroll, you're welcome to go, all expenses paid. What do you say? Want to go? You'd better say yes."

"Three days?" I repeated.

"No, I would only go for two, Saturday and Sunday," said Randy.

"This is a small show Del; it occupies four floors of the hotel. We could cover the entire show in less than two days. This craft show is located at the Reserve Hotel on the outskirts of DC. We could leave here early Saturday morning, check in to a hotel nearby, and do some shopping for the store. We could then see some of Washington, do some personal shopping, and head for home late Sunday afternoon. Interested?" Randy asked.

"Hell yes, I'm interested," I replied. All the while my heart began to do flip-flops and the flamingos were at it again. "But I have to check with Patti and see if she has any objections. Would Debbie be agreeable to this?"

"Yeah," replied Randy. "I go to all these shows for my dad because of his health. Deb is used to it; sometimes she has her mom come out spend the weekend with her and the kids, but not too often. You know how women are."

"Let me run this by Patti. I should be able to let you know tonight," I said.

"That's great!" said Randy. "There are two bigger craft shows coming up, and I'd love to have you go with me."

"When and where are they?" I inquired.

"One is in early October in Wilmington, Delaware, and the third one is in Pleasantville, New Jersey, later that month."

"Where the hell is Pleasantville, New Jersey?" I asked.

"Just outside of Atlantic City," said Randy.

"Give me the dates for each craft show and I'll see how Pattie reacts," I said. Randy jotted down all three crafts shows, where they were being held, and the dates.

"We would drive to DC, and maybe drive to Wilmington too, depending on the weather. But we'll fly to New Jersey. All paid for by the store of course, which would include hotels and meals," said Randy.

"You know that I would say yes right now," I said, as I gently squeezed his knee. "But I have to check with the boss and see what she has to say. And. I have to make sure that my office manager will work while I'm off. We rarely are open on Saturdays, so that shouldn't be a problem."

My heart was racing and the flamingos were doing a war dance in my stomach. Three weekends with Randy! I can't wait. Now how can I convince Patti to agree to my going? That's the problem. God, I want to go - I have to go!

Randy brought me back to earth with another drink, here's wishing you good luck with your wife letting you go to the shows."

"Thanks," I replied, "she might not even care. I'll find out later when I get home."

After dinner, when the dishes and homework were done, I approached Patti about the three craft shows coming up, explaining Randy's offer to me to learn the business by going.

"How serious are you about working at the hardware store?" Patti asked.

"Well, I really like the work; Randy and his father treat me as one of the family. I can almost set my own hours. Just so I'm there when they need me. Why do you ask Patti?"

"Well, if you really like it, and it looks like you love it, there could be a chance that you might buy into the business. If anything would happen to Big Ed, would Randy sell the store or continue to work it? If he wants to continue operating the store, in that case, he may want a partner to help him. Do you think he might consider you as a partner?" she asked.

"Anything can happen, Patti," I replied.

"But, would you be willing to quit Lamont and buy into the hardware store?" Patti added.

"Having the opportunity to work so close to home, be my own boss, and make some good money for this family - hell yes, I would do it in a minute," I answered.

"Well, go with Randy on these trips and see if you like this type of business," replied Patti, "Feel Randy out, see what his future plans are. Would he want a full time partner when his dad dies, or would he sell? If he would want a partner, would he consider you? If he says yes to these questions, then you have some serious thinking to do. You and Randy are real friendly now, but how would it be if you were partners?"

"You're right Patti; there's is a lot at stake here. I think Randy and I should have a pleasant chat to see which way the wind blows." Yippy, I thought to myself, I'm going on all three trips with Randy. I can't wait.

"I'll sleep on it Patti, and talk to Randy tomorrow," I casually replied.

Later, after Patti and I had made mad love, I rolled over to sleep, but my mind wandered. At last, Randy and I would have some quality time together. We usually sneak a kiss with the hopes that no one would see us or cop a feel when we felt it was safe. It's been hell trying to make out and have so many people always around, especially when we live next door to each other, with our wives and kids always around. We really couldn't do much. We tried going to Edgewater Dam after work but it was hopeless and dangerous. If it wasn't for the people there, it was the security patrol riding around looking for something to let them earn their money. We tried to make out at the dam one night and we couldn't even give each other a blowjob. It was the first time for both of us. I never did it before and when I tried, I had dry heaves and couldn't perform. Randy was worse than me, he gagged when he tried. So we settled for mutual masturbation. Then I dozed off thinking of us in a hotel bedroom, having wild sex. Oh, happy day!

It was about 10:00 a.m. when I arrived at the hardware store. I wanted to run into the store, grab Randy, hug and kiss him, twirl him around the room, and tell him that I could go to all three shows with him. Instead, I walked in as I did any other time saying good morning to Big Ed, nodding to Randy, and getting a broom to sweep the sidewalk in front of the store. When I returned, Big Ed was in the back of the store and Randy was watching me as I entered.

"By the way, Randy," I said, "make the hotel reservations for TWO for all the craft shows. I'm going with you."

"Are you serious?" replied Randy, almost shouting.

"Yep," I said," Patti agreed that I should go with you." Randy grabbed me and gave me a bear hug and I melted in his arms.

"What's all the racket about up there?" inquired Big Ed heading towards us.

Randy released his hold on me and told his father that I would be going on all three craft shows.

"That's great!" beamed Big Ed. "I'll have my two sons representing this store."

We had a great relationship, Big Ed and I. He's such a super person.

"I'll get the catalogues and you two can read up on what to expect," he said.

Randy grabbed my arm and gave me an affectionate tug. I got the message.

The next morning, I received a phone call at my office from Coach Wilson. He had been watching my son,

Eddie, ice skate and was very impressed with his natural ability. He then offered to coach him after school.

"ICE SKATE!" I exclaimed, "I thought he was into basketball."

"He is," replied Coach Wilson, "but he has been doing this on the side."

"How does Eddie feel about this?" I asked.

"Well, he thought you might be upset because he hasn't told anyone in his family. He really is good and shows a lot of potential. There's no charge for my coaching him after school, but if we were to go to an ice rink outside of the school, there would probably be a small fee to use the rink."

"Give me your number, Mr. Wilson. I'd like to discuss this with Eddie and his mom. I'll call you in a day or two," Del answered.

Randy wanted to know if there was a problem when I saw him later, and I explained what was going on. Randy then told me that Coach Wilson was coaching his daughter, Linda, and she was doing very well.

When I got home, I began the discussion with Eddie and Patti. I really had no objection to this if he really wanted to do it. But, Eddie said that he did want to do it. The coach was planning to have him skate with Linda as a pair. So it was settled. "He wants to do it, so why hold him back?" I thought.

Patti agreed too, but wanted to call Mr. Wilson to get some additional information. She was concerned about the possible costs involved. But the coach said that there would be no more immediate costs, just the fees incurred if they were to go to competitions. He further explained that a way to help defray those costs would be to get a few sponsors. Coach Wilson said he already has some people lined up, but it wouldn't hurt to solicit for more to help on our own.

CHAPTER 7 – Washington, DC

Time flew, and it wasn't too long before we were on our way to Washington, DC. We made an early start with the driving, leaving about 8:00 am. We arrived at the Reserve Hotel, checked in, unpacked what little clothing we had brought, and walked a block to the craft show. Before we left the hotel room, we had shared a few kisses, hugs and gropes.

I really enjoyed the fact that we didn't have to wear a suit. Our clothes for the show consisted of jeans, plaid shirts, V-neck sweaters, loafers, and sports jackets. Very casual, and I loved it.

An attractive young lady greeted us at the reception area, asking for the name of our company and our individual names. She gave each of us a packet, which included a pad and pen, and a credit card just to use for this show. The card read "Bishop Hardware," with my name and an account number beneath. Randy received the same. We were instructed to list everything we wanted to buy on our pads.

Each manufacturer had a partitioned area where they displayed their products. As you entered each area, there were several clerks stationed at computers to review the merchandise shown by the manufacture and process your order. Within seconds, you had an itemized list of what you purchased. We also received information about shipping, delivery, and billing. If an item was sold out, you knew when to expect delivery.

We covered two floors by 6:30 pm, and we were both tired and hungry. Randy wanted to call it a day, and I agreed.

It was a long day and I wasn't used to being on my feet all day in loafers. He reminded me that the show ended at 8:00 pm, so we didn't do too badly at all.

We crossed the street to enter a very large, clean and crowded restaurant where we had a great dinner with a couple of scotch and waters. We reminisced about what we had bought for the store while we had dinner. I think we bought some good items, a bit different for a hardware store. We decided to walk back to our hotel, where we went to our room, shed our clothes, and headed for the shower.

Playful is how I would describe our shower together. As we got ready to relax for the night, I put on a pair of briefs only to be chastised by Randy.

"Take them off," he growled teasingly. "When we get into bed, I don't want any competition."

"Okay," I agreed. "I thought I'd watch some television and have a drink or two before going to bed."

"You can do all that without briefs at all. I brought scotch, and there's plenty of ice. So, we are set for the night."

I walked over to the dresser and put my briefs back in the drawer. I was suddenly grabbed and pulled back onto the bed. And that was all she wrote. We were all over each other, kissing, feeling, and groping over and over again. We did pause for a while to enjoy our drinks, but then it started all over again.

Needless to say, my heart was beating rapidly and those damn flamingos - well they were going wild! I loved every minute of our lovemaking. Suddenly, Randy was using his tongue to lick my nipples, my chest, and stomach. Finally, he had his mouth wrapped around my hard cock. We had both tried this before, but it had been a failure.

The dry heaves we experienced were as a result of our inexperience. This time it felt like it was going to work, and it did! I exploded into his mouth and immediately swung around to put my mouth on his swollen cock. I pumped on him as he had done on me, and then he shot and shot until he went limp. We ran to the bathroom to spit out our newfound liquid.

Randy was elated that we both finally mastered the blowjob as it is commonly called.

"See," he said, "It was no good in the car because we were edgy, afraid of being caught, and of the scandal that might have followed us. Here, we were relaxed, and look at what happened."

We fooled around some more, then after watching the news; fell asleep in each other's arms. What a beautiful day and evening we had together.

I was up bright and early the next day; it was 7:00 am. Randy was still asleep, so I went to the bathroom, brushed my teeth, and saw that we had a coffee pot there with all the fixings, so I put on a pot of coffee. I used the remote to turn on the TV for the morning news, and slid back into bed with Randy. Just as I was getting comfortable, Randy woke up and went to the bathroom. After that, he brushed his teeth and used some mouthwash, and he returned to bed and snuggled up to me. After a few kisses, Randy asked if I enjoyed last night.

"Are you crazy? Of course I enjoyed it," and then began to laugh.

"What's so funny?" Randy wanted to know.

"I'm thinking about the first time we tried giving each other blow jobs and the trouble we had. I gagged, you puked, and I laughed. We felt that if any one saw us, we would have been arrested and put in jail."

I continued to giggle, but when he grabbed me, kissed me roughly, and slide down to put my cock in his mouth, it didn't take long for me to get hard. Randy didn't waste any time. He had me so hot in a few minutes that I shot before I wanted to. And, he kept it up.

"Randy, stop," I howled. The sensation to my cock was delightfully intense, to the point that I couldn't bear it anymore.

"Please stop," I whispered, "Randy, please..."

He finally stopped, saying, "Laugh at me, will you? I'll show you!"

Playfully, he kissed me again. Then I went down on him planning to get my revenge. Randy didn't take long to come, and when he did, I kept rolling my tongue around the head of his cock. I felt him shudder, his body stiffened, and he shuddered again. I knew that he was experiencing the same sensation, that same wonderful sensation that I had. But he wouldn't beg for me to stop, as I did. When his cock went limp, he withdrew from my mouth. After some playful moments, I told Randy that I had something to tell him.

"Tell me," he said, embracing me just a little tighter.

"Well," I started, "I wanted to make sure before I said anything to you. I feel awkward, but here it is - I think that I've fallen in love with you. I don't know how else to put it. I think of you all the time. When you walk into a room, my heart flips and those damn flamingos, well, that's . . ."

"What's so awkward about what you just said?" inquired Randy.

"I've never told a man that I love him, hey, that was clumsy for me to say. But, I wanted to say it long before now and never had the nerve."

Randy squeezed me a bit harder saying; "I've known it from the first moment I set eyes on you. I felt the same way, but I didn't want to scare you away."

After more love-making and passionate kisses, we decided to stop. The show was supposed to open at 8:00 am, and Randy felt we didn't have to open up the place. So we showered, dressed and checked out of the hotel. Then we took our bags down to the car and locked them in the trunk.

After a light breakfast, we were off for our second shopping day. We got there before 9:00 am and shopped the remaining two floors. We bought so many Christmas decorations - animated toys, lights, wreaths, trees, and garland. We also bought plenty of items for Thanksgiving. Randy and I found beautiful centerpieces, huge candles that were battery operated, animated toys and animals. Then, before we called it a day, we found an expansive booth offering hand-made jewelry. We were amazed at the quality and prices of such fine looking pieces. I saw Randy looking and admiring a slim, gold man's bracelet. I decided to buy it for him, which I did. My discounted price was one hundred forty nine dollars, it would retail for around four hundred fifty dollars, so Randy decided to buy me one and he did but we made sure that they were not identical, for obvious reasons. We also bought one for Big Ed that we would give him at Christmas. This was our first gift to each other but for all intents and purposes, we bought our own bracelets. We also bought tennis bracelets for our wives with their birthstones. These bracelets were exquisite. We bought all the kids pen and pencils set with their names engraved on each set. We had something for everyone, but especially our gift to each other, the gold bracelets.

Randy and I checked out of the craft show by turning in our charge plates and signing for all of our charges. We left the craft show and saw that we had some free time, so we took a walking tour of Washington for about two hours, and then we had an early dinner and headed for home around 5:30 p.m. On our drive home, I thought it was a perfect opportunity to ask Randy about his future with the store,

"Randy, if and when your dad should die, would you continue to operate the hardware store?"

"Yes Del," Randy said "I would continue to operate the hardware store. I have no interest in returning to my former job or work. I love the shop and want to continue to operate it".

I inquired about a partner, "Would you like having me as a partner?"

He almost went off the road. He pulled over and stopped the car.

"Del, are you serious about wanting to be a partner?" I said that I would like to work close to home, make a decent income for the family and to work with you, ..."Hell yes I'm serious."

"YES...I'd take you in a heartbeat for a partner," shouted Randy, "You're not just putting me on are you?"

"No. I really mean it. I'd love to work with you all day."

"What about Lamont Reality? You've been there for a few years, would you really leave them to work in a hardware store?" inquired Randy.

"Quicker than you could say scotch and water," I replied.

"It's a good job, but it's usually feast or famine. When the market is good, I fare out pretty well. When times are bad - it's not so good. When times are good, I usually put some money aside. I fare out well, but I could do better being my own boss."

It was a very happy ride all the way home. We arrived around 7:00 pm, and were greeted by our families and we sat down to give them their gifts. Everyone was happy to get something. The wives were ecstatic over the tennis bracelets. They couldn't believe how beautiful and expensive they looked. We explained what we had bought for the store. Debbie and Patti were surprised that we bought these kinds of items for a hardware store.

"Sounds kind of ritzy for a hardware shop," remarked Patti.

"That's what I thought," chimed in Debbie. "Do you think it will sell in the shop?"

"Well, we will soon find out. Everything will be here in about thirty days. We have to see if we have enough room in the basement to store the merchandise. I would like to keep as much of it as possible on the main floor to eliminate running up and down the cellar stairs," Randy replied.

"We also have to clear the windows in front of the store to make good display areas. I think that if we display the merchandise neatly and properly, it will help sell," he continued.

We were all in agreement that there was some work to be done. The wives agreed to help decorate the windows.

The kids agreed to run up and down the cellars stairs to get boxes and bring them up, if they weren't too big. It had just become a family affair for Thanksgiving and Christmas. Everyone was excited about the upcoming holiday season. We had lived on Belvedere Road for about four years. Randy's daughter was eleven, his son Josh was almost fourteen, my son Eddie was twelve and my other son Bobbie was eleven. They were old enough to help out in the shop after homework was done and on weekends. And of course they would be paid for their work. They couldn't wait. They were all happy and were hoping that they wouldn't have too much homework.

CHAPTER 8 – Wilmington, DE

It wasn't too long before the second craft show was coming up and we were making plans to attend. The weather had been good, no signs or forecast of snow, so Randy decided to drive to Wilmington, Delaware. This show was scheduled for Thursday, Friday, Saturday and Sunday. It was being held in the Armory and the same set up as before, only different companies. When we got there Thursday morning around 11:00 am, the place was crowded; it was a bigger show than the one in Washington. We had made a reservation with a nearby hotel before we left so we knew that we had a decent room. Wilmington is a clean, bustling city under the guidance of a wealthy family. We checked into the hotel, unpacked what little clothing we brought and decided to have sex before we hit the craft show. Later we entered the Armory, registered, got our ID's and began to shop. Some of the merchandise we had purchased in Washington but they had some new stuff that made your head turn. At about 6:30 pm, we called it a day and headed for a restaurant. After a leisurely meal, we walked around downtown for a while then headed for our hotel.

Once in our hotel room, the blinds were drawn, the TV was put on, our clothes came off and we began to enjoy ourselves. I was just so happy to be with Randy, to feel him, kiss him and make love with him; and I knew he felt the same way about me. He always smelled so clean and masculine. I've been meaning to ask the name of his after shave or cologne and keep forgetting. We couldn't keep our hands off each other. In a quiet moment, Randy softly said,

"You know, if you hadn't moved next door to us, we would never have met, we wouldn't be here right now. Fate meant this to be." And he kissed me again, while his hands were gliding over my body and my hands were active with his body too, I asked him what the name of his after shave lotion or cologne was.

"It's called, 'Follow Me', he said laughing. And as he continued to laugh, I caught on to his humor. I gave him a good smack across his rump. He laughed all the more. Then I pounced on him and we wound up laughing together as we rolled on the bed. I never knew that I could have such happiness with a man before. I couldn't explain it and I didn't want to explain it, so I dismissed it from my mind. He never did tell me the name of his lotion or cologne. We had another scotch and water, fooled around some more and finally went to bed for the night. We were cuddled in each other's arms when we fell asleep. In the morning, I was softly roused by a soft, sensual, sensational dream and I quickly closed my eyes to get back into the dream. I didn't want to lose this dream. I was suddenly wide awake when I realized it wasn't a dream. My eyes were wide open as I looked and saw that Randy was giving me a blowjob. I moaned softly, wiggled and gently turned due to the sensation I was feeling, and then, I climaxed. Randy had a towel and cleaned me before he said "Good Morning, Del."

"I like the alarm clock they have at this hotel," I replied.

Randy said that when he got up to take a leak, he saw me lying flat on my back with a ramrod straight hard on. It was too good to resist. So he took advantage of it. He didn't think I would mind. I told him I didn't mind as we kissed, then I grabbed him and when he was flat on his back, I went down on him. It didn't take him long to climax and as I used the same towel to clean him, I called him fast jack. He didn't understand the name fast jack. I explained that if he ever saw a rabbit having sex, it was over so fast, that they called the rabbit fast jack.

"You cum so fast, that I'm going to call you fast jack; and I wouldn't have you any other way. I really love you and could spend the rest of this day here in bed with you."

"I think we both know that we have a strong love here and neither of us want anything to come between us." Randy responded with a big kiss.

"I agree." So we fooled around for a spell and realized we had to do some shopping for the hardware store.

Randy and I did some shopping at the Armory, spent some money on decorations that were unusual and skipped several large displays that featured farm tools and accessories such as shovels, rakes, hoes, etc. We didn't live in a farming community and these items would never sell. We did find some interesting items for the housewife who has a little garden for flowers or vegetables. There were kneeling pads, half aprons with little pockets for small tools, and small watering cans. These items were good and very few stores have them for sale. It was almost 3:00 pm and we were getting tired, so we agreed to call it a day. We left the Armory and just walked around downtown for a while, doing some shopping for the family and us but not having much luck. Then Randy remembered that the hotel had a swimming pool in the basement that was open until midnight. But only one thing was wrong. We didn't bring bathing trunks, so we looked for a sports shop or a department store, found a sporting goods store, and they did have bathing suits. We each bought one, and happy with our purchases we headed to a nice restaurant for an early dinner. After dinner, we went to the hotel, changed into our bathing trunks, used the hotel bathrobes and headed down to the pool. We were the only ones there at this hour so the pool was ours alone. We did some diving, swam around the pool and just played in the water. It was very, very refreshing. As we were about to leave, several couples came down to swim so we left before it got crowded. Once in our room, we showered, put our bathrobes on, had a scotch and water, put the TV on and read some of the local newspaper.

Randy and I decided to cut Saturday's buying short, drive around Delaware, see some sights and just have a relaxing day together. On Sunday, we would attend church services, then check out of the hotel early, go do some last minute buying at the craft show, return our credit card and see how much we spent, have lunch and then head for home. I was in complete agreement; after all Randy was driving. In between this entire decision making, we were kissing, sucking and making mad love. What a wonderful trip this has been. I really didn't want it to end. Then Randy goes to the dresser and pulls out a bag, opens it and in his hand is a tube of KY Lubricant. He then explained what is meant by anal intercourse. I knew some of it. He felt we should try it tonight. It might be fun. Again, I agreed, I'd do anything with and for Randy. My love for him was growing stronger each day. Later that night, he lubricated me and very gently tried to penetrate me.

I screamed with pain. He quickly withdrew. I said, "Jesus Randy, the pain is awful."

To which he replied, "I haven't even got it into you yet."

"It still is very painful," I said, trying to hide the tears in my eyes.

"We'll wait a bit and try it again, it may be better the second time," Randy said.

A little later, he applied more KY and tried again, very slowly and very gently. Again, I cried about the pain and how it really hurt me. This time a few tears escaped my eyes and Randy saw this, he grabbed me and kissed me so passionately.

"Del, I don't ever want to hurt you." Believe me, I love you and want you to be happy with me. I would never do anything to hurt you or embarrass you. I'm so sorry, I thought that this might be good for us. We won't do it again." followed by a series of deep kisses.

I said that I wanted to try it on him; he may be more responsive than me. He didn't want to, but I insisted that he give it a try, he might like it. Reluctantly, he agreed.

Later, when I had calmed down, Randy agreed to let me try fucking him. I applied the KY generously and then I tried very slowly and as gently as I could to penetrate Randy. He really screamed into his pillow and he told me to take it out and get off him, which I did as quickly as I could. I realized that I had penetrated deeper into Randy than he did me. We both decided at this point, we did not like to be fucked in the ass. We both hated it and agreed we were happy with the sex we have had between each other and would keep it that way. I wondered out loud if maybe we were doing it wrong.

"I don't care if we were doing something wrong, it hurt like hell and I don't like it and I know that it hurt you too." "We won't do it again," Randy snapped.

We shared some kisses, cuddled each other and fell asleep watching a movie on TV. We woke up about 1:00 am, got ready for bed, had some sex and called it a day.

In the morning, Randy again expressed his apologies for the pain he caused me last night. I told him that I was equally as responsible. I know that I caused him some severe pain. We agreed never to try it again. After some loving and kisses, we went out for some breakfast.

During breakfast, Randy was very serious when he said," "I've been thinking Del, having you as a partner in the shop would never work." My heart stood still and I froze.

"Why not?" I inquired.

"Because, having you around me all day long would be a disaster. I wouldn't be able to keep my hands off you and I'm sure I speak for you too. We'd never get any work done. Who would wait on the customers?"

"Damn you, you had me believing you for a minute." My heart stopped beating for a minute, when I replied, "We'll manage to make a few sales."

We both laughed at his startling revelation. Randy was true to his word. We did some craft show shopping, left the Armory in the early afternoon, then decided to drive around Wilmington, sightseeing.

As it began to get dark, we went back to the Armory, parked the car and had a great dinner at a nearby restaurant. We had a full day and were beginning to feel tired. Once back in our room, we stripped our clothes off and settled in bed for a night of movie watching and lovemaking. I hated to think that this was our last night in own special Shangri La. I didn't want this to end and yet I knew it had to. We both had wives and children waiting for us back home. Randy and I couldn't ignore them. We both loved our wives and our children and would give our lives for them. But this, being here with Randy, was something else. As much as I loved and cared for my family, I couldn't get enough of Randy. My love for him was something I couldn't explain. And to be truthful, I didn't want to explain or understand what was happening. I loved him and wanted to be with him. I couldn't wait for the day that we would be partners. Don't misunderstand, I loved Big Ed and wanted him to live forever, but I couldn't help thinking of the day when Randy and I would be working side by side. Someone sucking my nipples and sending chills down my spine brought me back to reality. We spent a wonderful evening making love and doing things to each other that we both loved. Neither of us mentioned our sorry attempt at anal intercourse, but we both knew that we were sore and painful. Randy, in his wisdom, stopped at a drug store and bought some cream to be used for our pain. It was of little help. We were both still hurting a little in the morning.

CHAPTER 9 – Home Again

O n Sunday, after church and breakfast, Randy and I made a quick tour of the Armory, saw nothing new to spark our interest and then we checked out after receiving our bill. We were told that all merchandise would be shipped by the end of the week. We were on the road headed for home around noon. The ride home would take about two to two and a half hours. It was a pleasant afternoon so we enjoyed the ride and the trees changing colors. Randy and I talked about what we had bought for the shop, the big question… do we have room to store all that we bought? Randy felt that we would have enough storage room in the store by clearing all the little arrangements from the center aisle and making room for the new merchandise. First was Thanksgiving, then Christmas. He would like to keep out of the cellar with the new merchandise. We don't want to run up and down steps during this holiday season. If that didn't give us enough room, we both had nice size garages. We could store some things there.

"We are in good shape, I think," said Randy.

When we got home, the kids were our welcoming committee. They squealed and made us feel like were gone for a few months instead of a few days. We took our bags into Randy's den where Patti and the kids gathered. The kids were anxious to receive what we brought them, so we passed their gifts out first. Each got a game for their age bracket and a wallet with their name engraved on the outside. Linda got a small purse with a change purse inside and her name engraved on it. They all loved their presents and began to compare the games. We gave our wives their gifts. Each got eight sterling silver thin bracelets. We got two of each design. This is the latest fad and they are to be worn on the same wrist, it gives the impression of one very wide bracelet. Again the wives were very happy with our selections. Randy and I had bought genuine leather wallets for each other. For all intents and purposes, we each bought a wallet, but in reality, Randy bought me one and I bought him one. No one needs to ever know the truth. As we sat around talking about our recent buying spree, Debbie said that it sounds like you bought some nice items. Patti agreed.

"When will they be here?"

"The end of the week" answered Randy.

"Patti and I will check the stuff when it comes in," Debbie said. "We'll let you know if you've done a good job or not."

We all laughed at her grammar.

Debbie announced that you guys are going to New Jersey for another show in October…right?

Randy agreed, "October 17th, and it's for five days ending on the 21st. When we come home, we have got to get our ducks lined up to decorate the strip where the shop is located. It must be done before Thanksgiving."

"You have people lined up for that don't you?" Patti asked?

Randy said that we did but we want to contact them before they begin. We have plenty of time for that.

"I want to talk to dad tomorrow to see what we can do to make more space for the holidays," said Randy. "If we can get some of the junky stuff moved from the center aisle, we would have lots of room there."

Patti, the kids and I were walking across our back yards to go home, when I had some strange feelings that I never had before; jealousy - and envy. In the many months that Randy and I have had strong feelings for each other, I never had jealous and envious feelings. I did not want to go home. I wanted to be with Randy. It really hurt me to leave him alone, without me. Yet I wanted to be with my wife tonight very much. What was happening to me and my feelings? I wanted Patti, and I wanted Randy, at the same time. I'll run this by Randy; maybe he can explain it to me. I directed my total attention to Patti and the kids. As I drove to work in the morning, my mind drifted back and forth to the wonderful weekend I just spent with Randy. Just thinking about him started the flamingo birds dancing in my stomach. The office was functioning as though I had never been gone. This proved to me that I could be gone for a lot longer period of time and they would survive. Around noon, I was bored and left for the day. I called Randy and told him I was headed for The Lounge and he agreed to meet me for lunch. During our lunch, he told me that Big Ed has hired a carpenter to come in and make some center display counters; one large counter with three shelves leading to a top shelf. The three shelve would be like steps leading to the top shelf. It would be the same on both sides. It will be painted very pale blue and should be ready by the end of the week.

I asked, "What about the bins of stuff down that center aisle?"

"Dad is going to advertise a sidewalk sale for Saturday and Sunday. He feels the four kids can handle the sale and we will be around if there is a question about anything. And get this Del," continued Randy, "the kids don't know this, and we may not tell them, but whatever money they take in from the two day sale, is to be divided four ways and each one will get his share put into a bank account for them"

"Randy that could be a nice little sum for your dad." Why give it to the kids?" I said.

"Dad has always said," answered Randy, "you and Del are my only family. Del's wife is another daughter-in-law to me and all four kids are my grandchildren. You are the only family that I have. What am I going to do with it? Let strangers get hold of it? No way. The junk they are going to sell is what I inherited when I bought the store. No one wants it but people are attracted to a sidewalk sale.

Whatever they take in… it's theirs. I'll give them some money to make it worthwhile, but the rest goes into the bank for later on. We'll surprise them."

"Am I supposed to know about this arrangement?" I asked.

"Yes, Debbie, you and Patti should know about the bank accounts, but not the children."

"I can live with that", I replied.

Randy and I ran over most of the things we bought for the store. Big Ed was impressed and said that he was glad he decided to make more room down the center aisle.

"We'll need it, I'm sure. And I know that you are going to buy more from the New Jersey Craft Show. Hey, that's less than two weeks away. Are you ready for it?" Randy answered, "All we have to do is pack a bag. He already ordered our plane tickets, and made the hotel reservations at the same time.

"All we have to do now is show up. We're ready."

My heart did few flip-flops and the flamingos were at it again I have been counting the days until we could be together again. I can't wait. Oh happy day…! I decided not to ask Randy about my jealous feelings until we were alone in our hotel room. I don't even know what hotel we're staying at. All I know is that we are staying in New Jersey, near Atlantic City. I have left everything up to Randy. But after thinking about it, I really didn't want to fly. It's about a three or four hour drive by car. I mentioned this to Randy when we were alone.

"I thought that you would want to fly," said Randy. "I really don't care; I can drive if you would rather do that."

"Would you really mind driving? I can help drive when you get tired," I said.

"Hell no… We can stop when we want to get a coffee - whatever."

"Thanks. I really can't wait until we leave." I squeezed his buns and said, "We will be together for five whole days. Oh happy day"…

Andy came over to the hardware shop and wanted to know what would be a good day and time for the decorating guys to meet and measure and get an idea of what they would need. Randy and I agreed that Saturday would be a good day to meet and let them measure. However since we will be on a shopping trip for the store we wouldn't be back until October 21st so they had better plan the meeting on the 27th. We will be here then and most the guys could be free on Saturday.

"No problem" replied Andy that will give those girls time to get ready for the meeting.

"Who are the fellas Andy?" I inquired, "We have never met them."

"Well" replied Andy, "There is Gene Lahore who is about twenty eight years old. He works for the Tri-County Decorating Company downtown. He hates the name Gene so we changed his name to Frenchy and he loves it. He is pretty sure that his boss will give him a discount for some of the stuff he buys. Then there is Danny Roberts, age twenty seven. He is a bartender at a gay club called Uncle Mary's. It is a real hot spot in town. And then we have Lou Schmidt, who is co-owner of a card and gift shop downtown near the gay section of town. Joey Adams is the last one. He is twenty three years old and does not work. His mother died and left him well off. He gets an allotment, as we call it, each month from her lawyer. It pays his rent, buys food, clothing and gives him spending money. If anything would happen that he needed money or had to be hospitalized, he would be covered financially. So he works when they need him at Uncle Mary's. When he turns thirty, he will get the entire money momma left him, and I understand it is quite a bit. He is a nice guy in spite of his life style. So that's the motley crew. They are all nice guys or I wouldn't associate with them."

"I'm sure that whatever they do to decorate this strip will be a vast improvement over what we've had to put up with since I've been here", said Randy.

"I can't wait to see what they will do."

"I'm the new kid on the block, so I can't talk" and I winked at Randy.

Andy suggested that we all go out to lunch. There's a new Italian place opened near where I live called Pasta Palace. Randy checked with Big Ed who didn't want to go, claiming he would stay at the shop with the two girls. So we all headed to Hamilton Plaza where the Pasta Palace was located. It wasn't in the Plaza, but just outside of it and the lunch crowd was pretty good. Lunch was great. After lunch, Andy invited us to the building where he lived, Embassy Suites. There was an Embassy Arms right next door to the suites. The same man owned both buildings. The ground floor of the Suites had a large upscale restaurant. The ground floor of the Arms was a very nice upscale cocktail lounge and piano bar. In the center of the two buildings was a large hotel lobby. You could leave the piano cocktail lounge, walk through the lobby and enter the restaurant or vice versa and never leave the building. At the piano bar, we were seated around a smart table near the piano player, a woman of about forty who played show tunes.

Andy said, "She comes on about 11:00 am, then at 4:00 pm a man comes on and he plays regular cocktail music until 9:00 pm, when another man comes on and plays until 2:00 am. Everyone who can or thinks they can sing comes in here after 9:00 pm and they crowd around the bar and sing until the bar closes at 2:00 am.

When I'm here, I have a ball. It's so much fun to be at a piano bar... with all the drunks who think they are singing but really screaming. I'm kidding, there are a few really good voices singing. You guys ought to come up one night. You would have a good time. Bring the wives."

While we were sitting and drinking our scotch and water, a group of men walked by our table headed for the lobby. They were a really a good looking group of men. As they passed our table, several nodded to Andy. One leaned over and said something to Andy to which he replied "Yes, all night". They kept walking and the same young man said, "When I get back - OK?" Andy nodded approval and they were gone into the lobby.

"What was that?" asked Randy.

"That" replied Andy "is our Soccer Team. The coach has them stay here when there's a game coming up. The sporting complex is about three miles up I-95. They go up there to practice. A jitney picks then up from here and brings them back here after training. They are a nice bunch of guys."

"You know them?" I asked.

"Sure I know them. I usually get a drink or two here every night and they are here, so naturally we have become acquainted."

"Andy, how well do you know them? I saw that one leaning over and give you a message," probed Randy.

"Well, let's say that their cocks have crossed my lips."

"WHAT was that you just said?" I inquired, almost shouting.

Andy took a sip of his drink and said, very politely,

"Their cocks have crossed my lips. In other words Junior, I have sucked their cocks. Not all of them, but a lot of them. The one you saw whispering to me is a very happily married man with three children and he needs to be serviced tonight, so he will call me when he gets back, and we will both sleep well this evening."

"He's a married man?" Randy exclaimed, "And he comes to you to be serviced."

"Give that man a cigar;" Andy chirped. "He hit the ball right on the head."

Randy admitted that he was surprised. Married men usually go home for that sort of thing.

"Not when they are not near home," said Andy. "You know, most of my tricks are married men, you would be amazed of how many of my customers that I service sexually at the barber shop are married men. And their main concern is that I don't let on about them. They are petrified that their wives or friends will find out, then what? The soccer players don't want to fool around with hookers either. Think about it, they have to go and find a hooker. That means dinner, a hotel room and payment for services rendered; and if they find a hooker that doesn't want to be wined and dined, they want more money up front. And if the players are recognized, it could mean more trouble. Hookers want money to keep quiet, or else. Married men feel the same way. Unless they know you, they won't play. I've been sucking the soccer team for well over a year. No complaints at all. There are four married men and I suck them anytime they need or want it. The rest of the other players are single and they either have a girlfriend on the side that services them or they masturbate. Don't misunderstand, I have sucked most of the single men too, maybe not as often. As I said, married men feel the same way about the hookers. It's costly and they don't want the involvement. They come to me for ten - fifteen minutes - and it's over, no strings, no money, and no worry. It's the same with the customers in the shop. No strings, no money, no worry. What is great about this, I don't have to cruise looking for a trick. When these guys get horny they call me. One thing about a gay guy, he may brag about his tricks but he will never, never give out names. I love it. Now you know most of my secrets. Now, let me ask you a question... Are you two an item?"

"What do you mean by 'an item'" Randy asked?

"I mean are you two fucking each other?"

I froze! The adrenaline shot to my heart and goose pimples were on my spine.

"No, we are not fucking each other, Randy angrily replied (and he was being truthful). "We are both happily married, live next door to each other and Del and I are best friends. Our wives and children are close friends. Why would you ask such a question?"

"Well, you're both handsome as hell and when two handsome men are together as much as you two are, in the gay world, you're an item. No offense meant... I just had to ask.

"Let me ask you something Andy, while we're on the subject, do gay men fuck each other all the time?" I asked.

"No", replied Andy. "A lot of them do, but a lot of them don't. I personally don't like it. I was in my twenties when a handsome sailor let me pick him up. When we were in bed with me sucking his huge cock, he flipped me over and plunged that big thing into me. I screamed with pain and then he realized that I was a virgin back there. I was in pain for almost two weeks. Ever since that time, I let it be known to those who want to fuck me "That an exit back there, not an entrance. Of course there are exceptions to every rule. Then I met Dave. Dave is a very handsome Sergeant in the Marines; the man of my dreams. One night, the guys and I were carrying on at Uncle Mary's. The bar wasn't too crowded the night I met Dave. He was at the other end of the bar drinking alone and wearing civilian clothes. Next thing I knew, he had moved down to join us, bought a round of drinks for all of us saying that he hoped we didn't mind him joining us, but we were having so much fun that he felt he wanted to be with us. He singled me out to sit next to and to talk to. That's when I found out that he was a Marine and on a three-day pass. After a few more drinks, I began to feel the liquor and Dave wanted me to come to his hotel room for a nightcap. I knew what that meant so I agreed and went with him. Well, I fell madly in love with him as soon as he took off his clothes. He is the most gorgeous guy I have ever seen, and I had his ass on that bed sucking his cock. I couldn't get enough of him. Well, he wanted to fuck me and I froze. He felt me get rigid and tense, so I explained what happened to my sailor friend and me. He was so sympathetic and told me that the sailor was all wrong. He begged me to let him try and to do it the right way. Being under the influence of liquor, and in love with this handsome stranger, I agreed. First thing he taught me was how to relax my entire body. Then he began to ease into me very, very gently.

Well, it worked. We were together for his whole three-day pass and he fucked me every day and how I loved it and him. Every time he had time off, we were together. Then he got shipped overseas to the Middle East. That's been over a year ago and I haven't heard from him since. I gave him my address but not knowing where he was being sent, he couldn't give me his, but he promised to write to me. I think he really cared for me. So, I have let a few, VERY few, fuck me. I could count them on one hand. I really don't like it, but Dave...I really loved him, he taught me so much. God I wish he were back here again. And there are many, many men who don't like it. These people, like me, don't mind or get tired of giving a good blowjob or getting one. But in all honesty, I must say, my friends all claim that when fucking is done right, there is no better sex in the world. And after Dave, I must agree with them. Remember, the sailor hit me with his ramrod and I was very sore for a while. My friends have all told me that if he been a little gentler and tender with me, I'd feel differently today. Had he used a lubricant, greased my asshole generously and greased his dick generously and gently eased it into me, very slowly and gently, I'd probably be walking around with a 'room for rent' sign back there. I take their word for it. I always say, 'TO EACH HIS OWN'. Does that answer your question?"

"Yes, thank you." I wouldn't look at Randy.

I looked at my watch and said, "I think we better head for home. Randy has to close the store I have some chores to do at home."

Andy hugged the both of us and thanked us for a great afternoon. As we left the piano bar, Andy took his drink and glided to the end of the bar where there was a very good looking young man sitting alone and looking lonesome.

As we drove back to the store, Randy said, "Did you learn anything today?"

"Yes, how about you?" I replied.

We both laughed at our recent conversation with Andy but we both realized he spoke the truth as far as our recent efforts were concerned. When we returned to the store, the place had two customers and Big Ed said it was a slow afternoon. Big Ed offered to let the girls go home early. The store usually closes around 5:00 pm or 6:00 pm on weekdays and 8:00 pm on Fridays and Saturdays. Sundays he is open from 10:00 am until 4:00 pm. Holiday schedules are different. When the girls left, Randy got on the phone and cancelled our airline tickets. Ed heard the conversation and wanted to know why the change and Randy told him that he made the reservation without asking me and that I really didn't care to fly. Ed agreed with me.

"I hate flying too. I don't blame you Del; you can do more and see more in a car."

"Well, I know when I'm outnumbered," Randy said grinning.

We all laughed. I was thrilled that I would be in a car with Randy and we could talk freely and enjoy ourselves for four hours each way. When Big Ed was out of hearing range, I grabbed Randy by his arm, pulled him close to me and I whispered in his ear, "I love you so much," followed by a quick kiss on the cheek.

"Tell me something I don't already know." Randy said as he smiled at me with a quick wink. There go those damn flamingos again tap dancing in my stomach. O Happy Day.

"Did you enjoy the piano bar last night?" I asked Randy.

"Yes, I did, it looks like a great place to spend some time at night when they are singing. Let's check it out one night and if it's a fun place, we'll bring the girls there."

"Sounds good to me, I'd like to talk to Andy some more about the gay world, yet I don't want him to get any ideas about us. He floored me the other night about us being an item."

"I don't think he knows anything, just fishing," said Randy. "We have to be very, very careful. I don't want anything to happen to us or our arrangement."

"I agree... nothing can upset our arrangement."
Randy added. "As much as I would like to have and call you
pet names, we can't afford to do it because too many people
are around us and we can't become familiar with each other
that way. It could be bad for us both." I agreed whole-
heartedly.

CHAPTER 10 - Pleasantville, NJ

Before we knew it, we were on our way to New Jersey, to a little town called Pleasantville, about an hour from Atlantic City. We stopped at a diner for lunch. The food was fabulous. Not only that, there were great looking pies, cakes, and pastries on display as we entered. New Jersey is known for its diners, and great pastries with many of them offering baked goods on the premises.

The craft show was being held in a huge, two story brick building, located several blocks away. Nearly two hundred merchants would be displaying and selling their products. The show was not open to the general public; we had received an invitation to attend.

We pulled into the bed and breakfast that we had booked until Sunday. After checking in, registering and getting our packet including our charge card, we decided to take a walk around town. We found an Italian restaurant along the way, checked out their menu, and decided to have dinner there. It turned out to be a good choice. On the way back to the guesthouse, we picked up a bottle of scotch. Tired from the long drive and walk, it was time to call it a night.

When we got back to our room, I asked Randy whether he cared if we didn't attend the craft show on its opening day.

"No, he replied. It's open for five days, so we have plenty of time to shop. Many of the firms that attend only stay for the first day or so. Relax, it's okay to miss opening day."

"Glad you said that," I said, "because while we're here, I'd like to go to the casinos in Atlantic City. Are you game?"

"Wherever you go-est, I go-est," Randy quipped.

"What the hell kind of language is that?" I asked.

"It's from the book of Ruth!" You didn't recognize the biblical reference?"

"Is that what it was supposed to be? I thought it was Pig Latin or some other crap you picked up in your travels." I threw a pillow, and hit him dead center in the face. He wasn't expecting it. But then again, I didn't expect him to grab me, throw me down on the bed, and begin kissing me all over. And so it went, all through the night. We enjoyed taking each other's clothes off, then making love to each other. I couldn't have been happier.

"I have a tube of KY jelly with me," Randy said.

"Should we take Andy's advice and try it again, or let it ride for another time?"

"I'm content to let it ride. But what would you like to do?" I asked.

"Well", said Randy, "I wouldn't mind trying it again while we're on the road and not at home. Would you like to try it again?"

"Yes, I would, but if it doesn't work this time, let's forget it."

"Sounds good to me," said Randy, "but, maybe tomorrow night, Okay?"

"Okay."

We made ourselves a scotch and water. Lingering over the drinks, we were feeling relaxed, warm and comfortable. Randy and I snuggled and kissed, then fondled and caressed, when my hand found Randy's beautiful, muscular ass. Before I realized what was happening, he applied the KY jelly in and around his anus. He grabbed my hardened cock and smoothed a generous amount all over. Then, very, very gently Randy lowered his body onto my hardened cock. I could feel myself beginning to enter him. Randy rolled over and held my body with him. At that moment, I remembered Andy's advice to enter slowly, very, very slowly. Randy was pumping the bed ever so gently. I could feel myself going deeper and deeper into him.

"You okay?" I asked.

"Yes," he whispered softly. I was almost lying on top of him, afraid to move. I didn't want to hurt him, but he continued to pump the bed slowly and before I realized it, I was into him as far as I could go. My God, I realized I was fully into Randy.

"Are you okay?" I asked again.

"Yes," he said. Then he asked me to pump him gently and slowly, which I did.

"Faster, faster," Randy said not much later. I complied and he began pumping the bed faster and faster still. Within a few minutes he buried his face in the pillow and cried out, "I love you" and shot all over the bed.

At the same time, I exploded into Randy and repeated, "I love you too." We lay there for a few minutes limp and wasted. Randy twisted himself and gave me the best kiss he could muster in that position. I returned the kiss and grabbed a towel to clean us both as we lay there.

I asked Randy how it was and he answered that penetration was a little uncomfortable at first, but as we progressed, he didn't mind the discomfort.

"You were hitting the prostate or something, and I wanted to feel more of it. That's when I asked you to go faster, and when that wasn't fast enough, I began to pump, and that's when we both climaxed," he said.

Randy was lying very spent on the bed. I reached his ear with my mouth and asked, "Are you sure you're OK?"

"I never felt better in my life. What a feeling, I never had a feeling like that before. You're next. Not tonight, but tomorrow night you'll get yours," Randy promised.

"We'll see. Well, so much for trying this sex another night," I quipped.

"Well, we both had a few drinks and were feeling kind of mellow. I was so relaxed," explained Randy, "When you slid your hand over my ass, it sent chills up my back. I thought, what the hell, let's try it and see what happens."

"And look what happened," I added. We showered and continued our petting and love making until we both fell asleep.

Thursday morning we awoke, took showers, had breakfast and walked down to the craft show where we registered. It was the same procedure as before. Randy and I decided to skip the Atlantic City trip today, do some shopping, and go gamble on Saturday. We were given floor plans so we could easily find which crafts or stalls we wanted to visit. There were many stalls or units showing the same merchandise we had purchased earlier at the other shows. This was geared to furniture, lamps, rugs, leather goods and fine jewelry. There was a big display of washers and dryers, vacuum cleaners, detergents, kitchen supplies, etc. We didn't buy too much on Thursday. What we saw wouldn't sell in a hardware store, but we kept looking. Then we saw some bathroom accessories in a variety of shades and designs. We bought many things in butterfly patterns, bamboo, and all kinds of flowers. For the man's bathroom, we bought dog and bird patterns, ships, astrologer's stars, space ships, and shooting stars. There was something for everyone.

Randy and I skipped lunch and when we left around 4 pm, we decided on an early dinner. We found a neat looking restaurant called 'The Broken Blue Bell'. They had a great seafood menu, which satisfied both Randy and me. We had a very leisurely meal with a few drinks and we left the restaurant to walk around and see some sights.

When we began to get tired, we headed back to our Bed and Breakfast, where we planned to spend the night. We looked over what we had bought and how much money we spent. Randy wasn't too interested in how much we spent. He had a set figure in his mind and until we hit that mark, he wasn't too concerned. When the shades were drawn, we took our clothes off and had a bathrobe near the bed in case of an emergency. I always make a production of taking my briefs off and twirling them above my head; just to let Randy know that I didn't forget his sermon. Randy jumped up, caught me off guard and threw me gently on the bed; kissing any part of my body that he could get hold of and whispering,

"Make fun of me, will you me pretty, I'll teach you..." I couldn't stop laughing, and the more I looked at him, the more I laughed. "What the hell is so funny?" Randy wanted to know.

"You are." I laughed. "If you could see yourself... Are you're trying to imitate a gorilla?" I had to laugh again. "I wish I had a camera to take your picture, standing on the bed with your arms swinging, trying to scare me and then I look at your big cock and balls swinging back and forth." I couldn't stop laughing at this sight. Before I could say another word, he jumped on me and tackled me on the floor. After a few gentle, tickles and tugs, he kissed me on the mouth and we both stopped struggling. We both were kissing every part of each other's body. I don't know how long we were on the floor. Who's counting when you're having fun? Eventually he calmed down and let up on his monster act. I love this man. He was such a joy to be with. As I have said before, I can't get enough of him. We made drinks for us and put the news on the TV and just lay in bed, nude, loving and enjoying each other. Then Randy got very lovable and before long he got the tube of lubricant out and began greasing himself and me.

"Are you ready for me love?"

I mumbled a weak, "Yes, I think so."

"I promise I won't hurt you." I love you too much for that to happen" replied Randy.

Then he rolled me over on my stomach, spread my legs and slowly crawled on top of me. I felt the head of his dick slowly probe my cheeks. Then he very slowly and very gently begins to penetrate me I stiffened and braced myself for the pain I experienced the last time we tried this.

"Are you okay?" Randy inquired. I told him yes I was then he asked, "Why are you so tense and stiff?" I answered that it must be anticipation, from the other night when it was so painful. Randy said, "Relax, loosen up. I promise I won't hurt you." And while he's talking to me, he is sliding into me further and further, but ever so gently. I felt some discomfort, but nothing like the other night, and then I felt myself relax. After all, I love this guy and wanted to make him happy and I then totally relaxed my body. I began to feel some sensation and it seemed that the further he got into me, the better the sensation I felt, and the less the discomfort felt. I began to wiggle and pump very slowly. Randy picked up on my movements and began to slide into me deeper and deeper. Finally, he could go no further. Then I wanted more. I wanted him inside of me so badly and I could feel that he couldn't get deeper into me than he was. How do you tell your lover that you want him deeper inside of you and know that he can't do it? We both began to pump and thrash and my pain was drowned in the bliss that overcame me; I couldn't get enough of Randy and he could penetrate no further. I moaned and groaned, and finally, I came all over the bed and me. I turned as best I could and met Randy's lips head on. Then I felt Randy cumming inside me. The kiss was the climax to a wonderful sex act. We lay there for a few minutes regaining our breath and passionately kissing each other. When we regained our composure, we took a shower together, made some fresh drinks and had some discussion about the past two nights.

"Well," said Randy" What do you think of two men fucking now?"

"I never experienced anything like it before in my life. Never knew that my body could produce such ecstasy. I think that I'm going to love having this kind of sex with you. But where can we have it? We sure can't have anything like this at home, not with our wives and kids around, where do we go from here?"

"Well" replied Randy, "I've been thinking about that too. Edgewater damn isn't safe, so that's out. We could stay late at the store occasionally, but dad might get suspicious. The only thing I can think of right now is to rent a room and meet there. Well, let me give it some thought. We will enjoy our time together here and give some serious thought about the future. Right now, I want to love the hell out of you." He didn't get an argument from me. I can't explain the good feelings I experienced after having anal sex with Randy. We fooled around for a while, then watched a political thriller on TV, and after some more loving, we fell asleep around 10:30 pm.

Friday morning wasn't too clear. We were both a little sore from the fucking the night before but we didn't mind the pain as it was less than the last time we tried to fuck. It looked like rain but we had raincoats so we really didn't care. Randy had Friday all mapped out too. After breakfast, we would canvass all the stalls or booths that we had not covered. His plan was to get as much done as we could, even work a little later. Then have a good dinner and call it a night early.

On Saturday we could shower, have breakfast, make an appearance at the show and leave early heading for Atlantic City to gamble. They claim it is only about an hour's drive from here. We can spend some time there and come home before it gets too late.

"How does that sound to you?" Randy asked.

"You be the driver," I replied. I will be the passenger, boss."

He chuckled at my impersonation and ran after me in the bedroom but I reminded him, we were dressed and had a mission today.

"Okay but you're going to get it tonight," he growled

"We don't really have to shop today, you know," I tossed at him as I stood by the bed. "The bed is always inviting."

"You're right," he said glaringly. "We have work to do, but I promise you, your ass is mine tonight." Then he kissed me, rather passionately as we left for the day.

Once we entered the craft show, we saw some items that we never saw earlier. There was complete line of leather goods and some interesting costume jewelry. They also had several stalls loaded with candles of all shapes, sizes and fragrances. We bought plenty of these candles, as they would be a great for the holidays. These stalls were off the main path and slightly out of the way. We did buy some masculine items.

CHAPTER 11 - Atlantic City, NJ

Within two hours we were on our way to Atlantic City. Route 40 took us through all the little towns and boroughs, cornfields, small farms and greenhouses that you could see. It is a very clean state and one that you would want to come back to. I broke the silence of our ride with,

"When we get a chance, stop at a drug store, please."

"Sure, what do you need?"

"I want to get some condoms. I'm almost out of them at home."

Randy cried,"Del, you still use condoms?"

"Hell yes", I said. "Patti won't let me touch her unless I'm wearing a condom."

"How long has this been going on?" asked Randy.

"Right after Bobby was born," I answered. "She had some problems when Eddie was born and then with Bobby, it had to be cesarean section, and she vowed after that she didn't want any more babies. She even threaten to cut my penis off is she got pregnant again. So when we have sex, I need a condom, and if I don't have any, there's no sex."

"Well, I'm in the same boat. Debbie had two children and she let it be known there would be no more," Randy laughed. "She talked me into having a vasectomy. Since I felt that two would be a fine family, I agreed. I'm fixed and cannot have any more children. Do you want to have any more children, Del?"

"No," I replied. "Two is enough for me, but my wife is strongly against any more kids so we're in complete agreement."

"Well then, why don't you have a vasectomy? It's done in the doctor's office and it is not painful at all. And you wouldn't have to worry about buying condoms all the time," explained Randy.

"What does it involve?" I asked.

"Well Del, you make an appointment with this doctor, go in, have a checkup and he gives you a date and time to report to his office. This is all done in his office. When you get there, they give you a dressing robe to wear and you take off your pants, shoes, socks and your briefs. It takes about thirty minutes, and they give you a local anesthesia. They go into your scrotum, cut and clamp the vein or artery that supplies your sperm. Debbie wanted me to have it done so badly, she made the appointment with the doctor and went in with me to make sure I had it done. My appointment was for 9:30 a.m. and I was back at work by 11:00 a.m., just in time for lunch," Del laughed...

"And you had no ill effects from it all Randy?"

"None what so ever. Think about it, you wouldn't have to use a condom, or worry if you have any on hand when you want to have sex with your wife" said Randy.

"And this doesn't affect your sex life at all?" I inquired again.

"No...once the procedure is over, your sex life in better than ever. If you're really serious about this, I'll make the appointment and go with you to hold your hand."

"Let me talk it over with Patti and I'll let you know."

"Do what you want, but why talk it over with her? Isn't she the reason you're thinking about having it done?"

"Yes, but we have always had an open relationship and this way she can't bitch that I've kept her in the dark. Don't misunderstand, I am going to tell her that this is what I'm doing for her; I'm not asking for her permission."

"Knowing Patti as I do, she won't mind, she'll probably kiss you for it," said Randy.

The outline of Atlantic City was forming in the distance. Again, Randy repeated,

"Del, if you're really serious, I'll make the appointment for you, take you there, stay with you until it's all over and bring you back to where ever you want to go. Believe me, it's a very painless procedure. No one will know about this unless you tell them. The whole procedure is probably less than thirty minutes. Then you're on your own"

"Randy, I'm really giving it some serious thought, I'll let you know."

We approached the building parking lot of the Windjammer Casino. This casino had guards on duty when you park your car and also when you leave. They are there to make sure you get into your car safely and leave the lot safely. The Windjammer made it a public policy to protect their clients from robberies of any kind. They built crossover ramps on the third floor for clients to enter neighboring casinos without incident; you could travel from one casino to another without ever leaving the building. Most casinos do this to keep the robberies and other crimes down outside of the buildings.

We both agreed to lose just so much cash between us to leave before it got dark. The casinos were beautiful and worth the trip to admire their beauty. Being lit up as they were; they were the jewels of Atlantic City.

I hit on a slot machine for $50, then began to play with their money. I didn't mind this at all. Randy, on the other hand, had played several machines. Just as he was about to call it quits, he hit on the poker machine for $200! He was elated but not for long. He began to put it all back into other machines, but his luck left him by then. My $50 was dwindling too, so I had had enough. I was ahead by about $17. Just then I heard Randy yell, and as I turned to look at his machine, I saw that he had hit again with a straight flush – he won $1,000! I grabbed his arm, took his paper printout and walked with him to cash it in.

"But" he complained, "I want to play some more."

"No" I said, "It's getting dark and I think we should head for home. Especially while we're ahead"

"Christ, you sound more like Debbie. I thought I left her home."

"You'll thank me in the morning, believe me, let's go home."

When we arrived in Pleasantville, it was very dark, but at least we got home safe and sound with $1,017. Randy was a little pissed for a while, but when we got home and he had some money to boast about, he felt better and didn't resent my butting in about his money or at least he didn't show it. We parked the car, walked across the street to a good restaurant, had dinner and retired to our hotel for the evening. In the middle of our love making, cuddling and kissing, I propped my head on my hand, and resting my elbow on the bed, I said,

"Randy, I have to talk to you."

"Shoot Del, I'm all ears."

"Well, where are we going with our relationship?

"What do you mean where are we going?"

"Don't misunderstand, I love being here with you. But when we're in a hotel, we can carry on like this anytime we want. What about when we get back to our families? What happens then? We won't have this luxury. You know we are never alone. If it's not the kids, it's our wives, and the store is like grand central station most of the time. I want to spend time with you - quality time. The kind of time we have had in the hotels. What are we going to do? Where can we go?"

"Del, I have been giving this a lot of thought and to be truthful, I don't have a solution. I don't intend to lose you or even think of it. I have you, and I want to keep you. I never, never, never want to lose you, or even think of losing you. But this isn't answering our present problem. There is one possibility, and it may be our only chance. You know that when you walk into the store, you can look from the front door all the way into the rear of the store where there is a tiny office. Dad has a little table there, a small apartment size refrigerator and his electric coffee pot. I've been thinking about this for a long time, before you brought it up. Dad has not been feeling that well lately and he has been told by his doctor to take a nap during the day. Well his reply has been, "Where would I do that?" And he's right …to a point. I'm going to have his little cubbyhole enlarged to hold an extra-large cot for him to take a nap each afternoon. Then I intend to have a large piece of glass on the retaining wall, only it will be a two-way piece of glass. You can look into it and see a mirror. Inside the office, you can look into the store and see what's going on without anyone seeing you. I really want this for dad so he can get his rest. He needs the rest. But, when you and I work late at night after the store is closed, we can make use of the bed and no one will see what's going on. How's that sound to you?"

"Sounds like I haven't given you enough credit," I replied. "Does Big Ed know of your remodeling plans yet?"

"No, not yet. I plan to tell him when we get back. He may protest, but I have his doctor on my side."

"Looks like you got all bases covered. Why didn't you tell me before now?"

"Well, why should we both worry about this? I thought I would worry and when the die is cast then I would tell you. I didn't want both of us to worry about the same thing. I didn't know that you were thinking along the same lines as me."

"Feel better now that you know?"

"Yes, I do," as I slid my body next to him to be a little closer and I whispered in his ear.

"I knew I didn't a pick dummy to fuck with," he replied. "You're right and don't you ever forget it", as he grabbed my cock and began playing with it. We kissed, sucked and fucked with each other until we fell asleep for the night.

The brightness of the room woke me at about 7-7:30 a.m. even though the blinds were down. I looked at Randy who was still cuddled in my arms as he slept. Somehow the sheet was pulled around part of us during the night. I pulled the sheet off of us and admired his body. He was truly a handsome man with a fine body. How could I have been so lucky? I kissed him on the lips, no movement on his part. Then I kissed his eyes, his nose and his lips again; still no movement. Then I sucked his nipples and worked my way down his stomach until I hit his navel; still no movement. I gently blew into his navel, nothing. Then I began going down further with my tongue until I reached his cock, there was still no movement on his part. Then, I slipped down to his balls and sucked them very gently. He had a semi hard on at this point. Randy was lying on his side and I gently pushed him on his back, which was easily accomplished. I then crawled softly between his legs, pushing them further apart and when I was in the right position, I put my mouth over his still semi hard cock. As I did this, I put both of my hands behind him until I had each check of his ass in each on my hands. Then I began to suck him, slowly at first and picking up speed as I went along. I also began to push his cheeks toward me and I got the pumping action that I wanted. His cock began to stiffen and when I felt his fingers slowly moving down the back of my head to my neck, I knew that he was awake. I picked up speed both with my mouth and his cheeks, and I felt the head of his cock getting firmer, almost like a piece of steel. I knew he was ready and as I ran my tongue around his cock head, it got harder and harder. Then it happened, as his body became very tense, the volcano exploded in my mouth. He had pulled a pillow to his mouth to stifle his climaxing scream. I didn't stop. I kept on rotating my tongue around his cock head and at the same time pulling his ass cheeks towards me. He began to wither, softly moan and groan but I didn't stop. I continued my course of action. Then he whispered,

"Oh baby, please stop. I can't stand the sensation." Still, I kept on. Then he tried to pull his cock from my mouth but his cheeks in my hands prevented that. I continued to swirl my tongue around his cock head until he pleaded with me to stop.

"Please, I can't stand it anymore." Then I stopped and released his cheeks, as Randy was limp on the bed.

"Good Morning", I said cheerfully. Did you sleep well?"

"Yes I did Del, and I have never in my life had a blowjob like you just gave me. Are you trying to kill me?"

I ignored his last remark. I guess if that sensation doesn't stop, you could have a stroke or a heart attack due to the sensation being inflicted on you. Instead, I asked him if he has had blowjobs like that before. I questioned him and he answered,

"Surprised? Hell yes" he almost whispered, "When I was in high school and college. There were some guys who gave blowjobs. But nothing like you just gave me. I love you so much. What did I do to deserve such treatment today?"

"Well" I said, "I felt that this will be our last day to share a bed together and I wanted to make it a very memorable day. I wanted to give you a special treat that you'd remember for a long time. I hate to think of sleeping in bed without you tonight or any other night for that matter. Maybe your plan for the remodeling of the store will help us out but until then I will have memories, or we will have memories. Was it enjoyable for you, seriously?"

"Honey, it was the best I ever had, as I said before. My dick is still quivering." And with that, he jumped me and began to suck my cock." He always does that to me. Gets me off guard and then jumps on me like a wild man...and I love it. Our lovemaking was wild but I think I got the best of him with my silent attack. We lay in bed, caressing each other, neither of us wanting it to end, but reality set in. We had a lot to do, so we reluctantly showered, got ready for church and after church, came back and had breakfast. Then we packed our bags, checked out of this wonderful bed and breakfast - which I will NEVER forget - put the bags in the car and went to do our final shopping spree at this show.

CHAPTER 12 – Back at the Craft Show

O nce inside the craft show, we headed for the last sections that we had yet to visit. What a surprise! Here we found bathroom accessories. There were all kinds of designs and patterns. Flowers, ferns, contemporary and futuristic patterns in addition to the plain solid colors. We bought a lot of these that we think will sell. Then we went into the kitchen area where there were so many designs, it made your head spin. The kitchen items consisted of four canisters, a cookie jar, salt and peppershakers, foot pedal trash can, a blender, mixing bowls, etc. Each could be purchased separately or as a unit. The designs were strawberries, lemons, oranges, apples, all fruits, peppermint sticks, jellybeans and other candies plus green spice plants such as parsley, mint, sage, etc. Shelled nuts and of course, pasta. There were all shapes and sizes. The sets also came in a variety of colors. Everything was trimmed in chrome. They even had oriental figures and printing on some items. We spent a lot of money here. Randy and I were given a flip chart showing every pattern the firm made showing dogs, birds, ships, sports patterns for bachelors that could be ordered and guaranteed delivery in three days, if it was in stock. The flip chart was our big plus. People could see what was available and would order accordingly. As we left the display areas, we were given a catalogue featuring everything on sale in the building. There was a written guarantee of delivery for every item in the book. Most were for three days if the item was in stock. Delivery was one to three weeks for all other items. This book was to show customers what was available if it was not in the store. Using e-mail, the stock number and our store number that they had given us, would get quick results for delivery to our store.

Randy and I said our goodbyes to the few people we knew and headed down the road to an Italian restaurant for lunch. The weather was a bit cloudy, but no mention of snow; even though it felt like it might snow at any time. The trip down Route 40 included winding roads that made us pray that it wouldn't snow until we were on I-95. Our prayers were answered. It didn't snow at all. As we drove on I-95, we talked over the wonderful few days we had together and how we hoped to get together again... and soon. Randy had slipped and called me "Baby" and I slipped and called him "Honey". We both realized the slip and had to promise each other not to do it again. In front of our wives or children would be unforgiving. They need not know anything except the fact that we are really good friends, nothing else. One slip in front of anyone of them could mean disaster. We have got to be very careful. Randy and I both agreed to watch our remarks for each other when other people were around as well. While we were alone and could talk, I brought up the matter of me being resentful that he went home with his wife after our last trip. I explained the best I could about these feelings that I have had and can't explain. Randy told me that he has had similar feelings and tried to resist them. However, they keep coming back. He even thought about going to see a doctor. Maybe we should both go see a doctor.

"You're kidding, but I think it might help us both," I replied. Randy said to give it some more thought and in all probability, we will go see one.

"Speaking of doctors, I've been giving it some thought about the vasectomy. I think I'll do it, make the appointment and go with me. I would like an early morning appointment.

"What about Patti?"

"I'll tell her before I have it done, if not sooner. It's not important. I do intend to tell her."

Randy asked, "How soon do you want to do it?"

"Whenever," I replied. "I really don't care, but do it while I'm in the mood to have it done."

"I'll call Monday morning before you change your mind," said Randy.

Randy and I stopped at a road stand to buy some fresh veggies and fruit. While there, I saw a sign near a playpen that read "PUPPIES FOR SALE". I walked over and saw five of the most adorable puppies.

"Hey Randy, look at this" and I motioned him to come over and see these cuties. When he came over, he fell to his knee and began to play with all of them. One was white, one was beige and the other three were a blend of white, beige and dark brown. All five were females and they were very playful and spunky. We played with them for about ten minutes and the owner came and joined us.

"Cute dogs aren't they," he asked? We both agreed.

"What breed are they?" asked Randy.

"Well, their mother is a pedigree Chihuahua and I can see Jack Russell in the White one, and some Pug in the beige one," said the owner. "But the other three, only God knows what they are. So I'll tell you what I tell everyone else, the father's mother had to be a tramp." We all laughed at that remark.

"What's the selling price and how old are they?" asked Randy.

"They are two months old and I'm asking $25 each. Now if they were full pedigree, I would ask $450 a pup and get it. "Excuse me for a minute. Some people want to buy some vegetables. I'll be back."

"We didn't get anything for the kids this trip. What do you think of a pet for them to call their own?" asked Randy.

"I don't know Randy," I answered. "How will the gals feel about a dog?"

"I won't mind; I always had a dog. Dogs and kids go together."

"Let's do it," said Randy. "The kids will be so happy."

"I might get thrown out of the house and have to sleep at your house tonight" I replied. "That might not be too bad of an idea, Del, think you can arrange it?"

"Yeah, sure, I'll wave a magic wand and say 'poof', so be it." The owner came back and Randy told him that we would take the two dogs.

"Could we have a box for them to travel in?" The owner agreed and said he would put an old towel in the box with some food and a dish for some water. I picked the white one and Randy took the beige one. Both were female dogs and litter-mates. They should get along fine living next door to each other. They were good as gold going home. They slept most of the way. When we drove into Randy's driveway, the dogs were still sleeping so we let them be; we quietly took our bags out and went into the house to meet our families.

CHAPTER 13 – On the Job

The kids and Patti were at Randy's when we pulled in. We had bought each wife a cashmere sweater. They fell in love with them.

Then the kids began,

"What did you bring us?" The less we said, the more they clamored for an answer.

"Wait, I left them in the car, I'll go get them," I replied.

When I returned with pups, the hollering and squealing got louder and louder. Needless to say that the pups were a big hit. You could not have given them anything better. Debbie smiled when she saw the dogs and said,

"Looks like our work is cut out for us, eh Patti?"

Patti replied, "It sure does. Well, we have to set some ground rules as to who does what around the house for the dog. Debbie and I will make a list of do's and don't's for the dogs. We'll do it while you're in school and when you come home, we can discuss them. Have you picked out names for them yet? No? We'll sleep on it and we can discuss it later on."

The dogs were the hit of the trip. We were all playing with the dogs when we had to break up the party. School tomorrow as well as our jobs. Then we were hit with,

"Can she sleep in our room tonight?" Patti spoke up and said,

"I don't know about Debbie, but I think our new house guest should sleep in the laundry room until she becomes familiar with us and the house. And when she makes a BM (Bowel movement) on the floor, who is going to clean it up? So before we get too attached, there are some ground rules to be set in place. She can sleep in the laundry room until these little items have been set in place. Okay Debbie?"

"Absolutely, we can all live with this arrangement for a few days. Thanks Patti" chimed Debbie. And that's how we left the first night with our new roommates

Morning came and saw the kids running around to keep their mother's happy and also to let the dogs know they were loved. And the kids would miss them until school was out. All of our back yards had a five-foot hedge around the property lines. Randy had removed a three-foot wide section between his yard and mine, this way we could all visit each other without going around to the front of the house. When Randy got to work, he called the carpenter who had put the shelves in, to come down the house and do some work for him. When he got there, Randy wanted him to install a two-foot high wire fence all around his yard and mine so that the dogs could play there without getting away. Even when the dogs are full grown, they would be too small to jump the fence, and if they did, they would hit the hedge head on and go nowhere. When Randy told me what he did, "I didn't think you would mind a safety fence to keep the dogs in. They can run freely in both yards."

"No, I don't mind at all. In fact I was thinking along those same lines myself."

"Now that scares me", Randy said. "We're beginning to think alike. It really does scare me. You know, this isn't the first time. On our shopping trips, I'd be thinking about buying something and you'd beat me to the draw. It happened three times in one day. You really freaked me out. I never said anything because I wasn't sure. I'm still not sure. Now this!"

"Hey," I replied, "I'm not physic or anything like that. And I sure as shit don't want to scare you away. I love you, and want you near me all the time. What happened is just a coincidence. Don't even give it another thought. Are we on the same wavelength? As I affectionately grabbed his arm."

"You bet we are, it's just so damn funny," said Randy. "Maybe it's a good sign and I'm too dumb to realize it." A little pat on the rear for Randy and the issue was a thing of the past. That pat meant so much.

When we got home from work, the girls had a system worked out and the kids loved it. Each of their rooms had a calendar on the wall. The oldest one in the room had to put his initials on every other day of the month. When their initials appeared on the day of the month, it was his or her turn to walk the dog in the morning and clean up if the dog made a BM. This way, someone had doggie duty every day. No excuses unless they were sick, then mom would take over. Mom would prepare food for the dog, but if your initials were on that day, you had to feed her. All the kids, and dads, were in agreement with this schedule. As it worked out the kids had a method of their own. Oldest child took all even days; the younger child took all odd days. They were happy that their mother let them keep their method. Debbie said it was easier than the system that she had worked out.

As Patti and I got ready for bed, we were laughing at how much responsibility the kids suddenly developed because of a puppy. The boys decided to call the puppy "Holly" because it is so near Christmas. Patti liked the name too. Randy's children decided to call their puppy "Cleo" after Cleopatra. They thought the names were cute and were especially happy that the children all named their dogs.

"Oh, by the way, I'm going to have a vasectomy performed." "Oh why?"

"Well, you don't want any more children, neither do I, so instead of risking a slip, I'm going to have the operation and then I won't have the worry on my mind anymore."

"Who is doing it?"

"Randy is going to make the appointment with his doctor. He will go with me."

"When is this taking place?"

"As soon as he can get me an appointment. "It takes about thirty minutes, and you can go right back to work and you can also have sex as often as you want, the same day. Almost unbelievable isn't it?"

"How safe is it Del? Many things can happen or go wrong. Is he a good doctor"?

"Randy had it done by this same doctor years ago and look at him, the picture of health."

"Well, if you think this is okay and it's what you want, then go for it."

"It is and I will, I don't expect any problems, and isn't this what you want too? Didn't you tell me after Bobby was born that you didn't want any more children? And you're now asking me if this what I want? I think the proper thing to say is that this is what WE want."

"But I want you to be certain."

"And if I am not certain, and decide I would like to father more children, who would I have them with, a hooker? I love you, love you very much and I want you to be happy; and if this will make you happy, so be it. Anyway, I wanted to let you know that I will soon be sperm free and will never have to buy another condom." We laughed together on that remark. Later, Randy told me that he called Dr. Izzy and I had an appointment for Thursday morning at 9:30 a.m. Also I should call his nurse and give her my insurance information.

"Not a problem," I replied.

Thursday morning rolled around so fast that I couldn't believe it; I could have sworn it was Wednesday. Dr. Izzy was a short stocky man, and must have been real looker in his day. He went into great detail to explain the procedure. He informed me that the operation takes about twenty five to thirty minutes, requiring a local anesthetic. A small incision in the scrotum and a minor surgery and it was all over.

"You could go back to work and continue your life as if nothing happened. However, when you leave my office, I will give you two envelopes, each containing 12 condoms. Every time you have intercourse, you must use one. When you have completed all twelve, come back and I will see if you are sperm free. If you are not, then continue to use the remaining twelve. Then come back in for another exam to see if you are now sperm free. It usually is successful after the second envelope." I asked what he meant by 'exam' to see if I'm sperm free?

"You masturbate into a glass. We check your fluid and if there are no sperm cells there, you're free to stop using condoms." He then produces a chart showing how he cuts into the sperm tube and clamping it shut. "The other part of the sperm tube receives your fluid and that is the tube where some sperm cells are sluggish and don't leave at once. By the time you have 24 ejaculations, the tube is clear, but we must be sure. At that point, you never need to use a condom again. Any questions?"

"None."

"Okay, let's get started. My nurse will prep you."

I followed her to another room where I put on a hospital gown and laid on a table. Randy was in the room waiting for me. He was going to watch the procedure. I was a bit apprehensive but felt better when I knew Randy was there. Before I could get too comfortable, it was over.

"Follow my instructions. If you have any questions or problems, call me at once, if not, I'll see you when you use the first envelope of condoms. Have a good day. Nice seeing you again Randy."

The whole procedure took about forty five minutes and I felt nothing at all. I couldn't believe it. Randy suggested that I take the morning off and have an early lunch. Big Ed knew what was going on with the vasectomy, so he knew where we were and that Randy might be a bit late.

Our lunch was really enjoyable. Anytime that I can spend time with Randy is "great" for me. I hated to see it end. Randy tried to talk me into taking the rest of the day off since I had a good "Medical" reason to do so. I said no, I really wanted to make sure the office was working efficiently in my absence. My staff knew I was having surgery today but not for what. I decided, with Randy's help, to lie and tell them I had a dangerous mole removed from my inner thigh. That way, I wouldn't have to show them the incision. I agreed to use his excuse, but I really had to get back into the office today. Randy's suggestion was very tempting, but I went to work. I could have taken the day off, Lynne had the place perking, and she thought that I wouldn't be in until tomorrow. Everything was under control, so I decided to leave early. I'd call Randy and meet him at The Lounge and have a drink or two, before going home. After Randy and I had our first drink, in walks Andy, who ordered a round for us.

"Glad you two are here. The guys are coming out this Saturday to size the place up, measure and take notes of what they will need. Do you have any money for them?"

"Holy shit," exclaimed Randy. "We haven't even thought about money for the decorations."

"Let's start collecting from everyone today and tomorrow so that we can have some cash when they get here Saturday," I suggested.

"Between the three of us, we should get it done," said Andy. "We'll contact the same people we did when we did the survey."

"Sounds good to me," replied Randy. We agreed to visit the merchants as soon as possible to collect money for the decorations. We enjoyed our drinks, had another round, then we all called it a day and went back to our shops before going home.

Saturday morning was here, bright and sunny ushering in a slight warming spell. After our coffee and donut break was over, the guys went outside to measure the roof, the walls, lamp posts and window spans. They came back in and big Ed had put a fresh pot of coffee on, and we continued the meeting. They agreed on all decorations being white and silver with all white lights and they were tickled with their choices, no red, no green, just white and silver.

"It will make it look so dreamy and frosty," drooled Andy. "People will love it." They planned on coming to the mall the 3rd and 4th of November, Saturday and Sunday, to decorate. The guys thought they could finish it in two full days. Randy and Andy collected $950 from the merchants before the decorators showed up. Most merchants were tired of the meager Christmas decorations they had put up with for the past few years. They were all ready for a change. The guys could buy what they needed and have the bills sent to Randy who would pay them. If they bought supplies and had nowhere to keep them, Randy let them keep it in his store's basement. It was amazing what they began to bring in the basement. The basement looked like a winter wonderland. Everything was white and silver with plenty of glitter. Then they began decorating the mall. The fun these guys had decorating was unbelievable. They had names for each other and insults galore; yet with all this bantering back and forth, there was a strong sense of camaraderie between them. Lou threatened to put Frenchy out of business when he zipped up his fly. Frenchy complained he could never find it, go ahead and zip it up. Danny said he found it once and wanted to sell it. Lou told him to keep quiet or he would tell tales about Danny. This went on for a spell, especially when the block had no customers shopping. The guys were making some progress, the white and silver garland brightened up the whole area. Then they decide to kid Joey who was working and saying nothing.

"Joey? Been on Route 40 lately?"

Joey's face got red and he said "no."

Andy wanted to know more about Route 40. Danny said that it is rumored around the bar, that Joey's tricks always take him to the motels on Route 40. It is also rumored that Joey can tell you what kind of wallpaper print is on the ceilings of any motel on Route 40.

"Is that true Joey?" Even Joey laughed at that one. I asked Andy later how Joey could know about the wallpaper on the ceilings. Andy said to me,

"You really are green, aren't you? Well, many men lay on their back to get fucked and while on their back, they can get a good look at the wallpaper on the ceiling." I replied that I didn't know they lay on their backs. Andy said, "Oh yes, when you're on your back, your legs are up in the air and the cock can go in deeper. What planet did you come from? You don't know too much about sex, do you?"

I replied, "Not gay sex, no."

Andy said "Well, from now on I'll have to take you under my wing and explain things to you." Frenchy heard Andy's lecture to me and said,

"Queen Mother is at it again... Better pay attention Del, she'll probably give you a quiz later on." And everyone laughed.

"Frenchy", Andy growled, "If you don't stop calling me Queen Mother, when you came down from that ladder, I'll whack your weenie," Frenchy roared and said,

"He whacks my weenie several times a week, no wonder it doesn't function right. Maybe one day he will feel sorry for me and give me a good blowjob." Again they all laughed. A bit later, I heard Frenchy call Andy and say,

"Andy, dig the jewelry on this girl walking towards us." I looked and didn't see any girl walking towards us. I saw a handsome young man, about twenty five or thirty years old, coming our way but I couldn't see any jewelry on him.

"Right on," yelled Andy. When they called it a day they all went to the Embassy Suites where they had a great restaurant on the first floor, right across from the piano bar. We all enjoyed our meal and had a great time carrying on with the crowd. In a quiet moment, I asked Andy about the girl with the jewelry.

"You didn't see her?"

"No", I said, "I saw a young man coming toward us but no girl."

"Jeez Del, I have to teach you a lot. The young man was the girl Frenchy was referring to. When a good looking or handsome man, or any man comes in our view, we call him a girl so if he hears us, he won't know we're talking about him. As for the jewelry, Frenchy was calling attention to the big bulge in his pants, his crotch. We call that jewelry. Sometimes they call it a big box, means the same thing. He has a big dick, worth looking at. If the bulge is in the middle of his pants, he's wearing jockey shorts. If his bulge is hanging to the left or right, he's wearing boxer shorts or no underwear at all. Again, he doesn't know we're talking about him but it's worth the time to look; and when we look, we are cruising him. Understand now?"

I laughed and said, "Now I do."

"Before I forget, said Andy, there's another side to this ball buster. If she doesn't show a box or jewelry, she may not have anything to show. Some people, believe it or not, are infantile. Some are growers, once you begin to get them arouse, they begin to show, but VERY small. Thus you have the growers and the show-ers. Most gay men love the ones who show it all." Gee Del, you are really naive. How about Randy? Does he know any of this?"

"If he does, I'm not aware of it," I replied. Just then Randy came out of the restroom after washing his hands. He joined us at the table and ordered a drink. Andy said,

"Look at the jewelry on this girl." Randy looked around, did not see any girl nearby. He then looked at his wrist and found his bracelet was not visible.

"I don't see any girls around here and if you mean my bracelet, how can you see my jewelry when it's under my sleeve?" I had to laugh now that I knew the language, and Andy said,

"It's not your wrist we're looking at sweetheart…it's your crotch. You're packing a big bulge there my man, worth looking at." I had to laugh at Randy and his reply.

"I never knew that there was a gay lingo." To which Andy replied,

"Christ, I can see I'm gonna' have my hands full with educating both you and Randy." I laughed at his sense of humor,

"I guess you never heard about buns either?" asked Andy.

"I don't think so. What you mean by buns," I asked. "Is that your ass?"

"You're not too dumb after all. When they say he has nice buns, they mean his ass. You, for example have beautiful buns, so does Randy. I wouldn't mind having either your buns or Randy's buns for breakfast. Tell me the truth Del, are you two fucking each other?"

"No, we're not." I said truthfully. Then Andy said,

"You two don't know how close you have come to having people grab your crotch or buns. That includes me... They're so damn inviting. You two are temptation waiting to happen. Maybe one day I'll get you both drunk and have a field day with both of you."

"Don't hold your breath on that one," I laughed.

Randy was still a little confused about the language having come into the tail end of the conversation, but not for long. I had the pleasure of explaining to him what they were talking about. Randy put his hands in his pockets and tied to adjust his crotch; but no matter how he tried to hide it, he still showed a big crotch. I winked at him; I didn't mind looking at his 'big' crotch... There wasn't too much he could do about his ass. I never complained about it or minded looking at it. As a result of Andy's explanation, I began looking at men and their jewelry or box. Very interesting.

Debbie and Patti knew we wouldn't be home for dinner because of the decorations. Meanwhile back at the store, the carpenters were there working on the room at the rear of the store, early in the morning. The small room with a door, and a window was shaping up. There was a cot, a small sink, a desk, table and a hot plate, and a closed in flush. All of the conveniences were to make Big Ed relax. The window and door, which had a small window in it, were both one-way glass whereby you could see out, but no one could see in. This was done for Big Ed, but Randy also had himself in mind. When we would be there alone, it would serve our purpose. When the store was closed and we would stay there, he would pull down a shade on the front door, the main entrance as he locked it and we would retreat to the back room. If anyone questioned it, he had a desk back there to do store business. Randy had it all planned, and it would work. I felt so lucky to have him in my life.

Day two found the guys on the job bright and early with their coffee and donuts. They were making good progress. Frenchy brought several frosted white poinsettias that his boss gave to him. He had the poinsettias for a couple years and no one wanted them, so he gave them to Frenchy to get rid of. He wanted to buy something else. When they were opened, they resembled a huge group of flowers and were to be used on the roof to drape the garland. They had enough to put one above each door on the strip. Frenchy was a good asset to the group. His boss gave him a nice discount on all the merchandise he bought. This was a big savings to the group. They placed a life sized Santa on the center of the roof with a spot light lighting him up at night. The spot light was on a timer that went on at dusk and off at 11:00 pm. Frenchy borrowed this from his boss. At each end of the mall were three large angels, each holding a white candle. The angels were made of white fiberglass material trimmed in faint, gauze like, shiny gold metallic material, with white lights under each skirt. All the lights were on the same timer, and there were hundreds of white lights all over the place. It really did look like a winter wonderland. All the store windows were trimmed with small white lights, each corner, by the drug store and food store was a very large tree completely decorated with white lights, and all white and silver ornaments. The garland was draped from the overpass above the sidewalk, which was all white and silver in three draping layers. They were also loaded with tiny white lights. The only color was the Santa on the roof. He was in his usual red outfit trimmed in white. The entire mall area was breathtaking and a joy to see. The merchants were delighted and passed on the comments of their customers. They had some decorations left over so they even put some glitter and white lights around the entrance to The Lounge and Beauty Shop. Back there it was so poorly lit and almost gloomy, that these few decorations brightened up the entire back of the buildings and made it inviting. The guys did a great job and the spotlight on Santa on the roof was drawing people to the mall that never went there. The merchants had or were doing their windows displays. Everyone was getting the spirit and all would be ready for Christmas soon. The bills were sent to Randy and they spent a total of $535. We had collected $950 from the merchants and The Lounge and Beauty Shop chipped in $25 each that totaled $1,000, deducted $535, leaving $465 for the guys to divide. Randy and I chipped in $35 which amounted to $500 for the guys to divide among themselves for their labor. They each got $125 and were surprised to get that much. They already volunteered to take the decorations down whenever we wanted them to, at no additional cost. It didn't take a Philadelphia lawyer to figure out that someone was making a nice profit on this decoration bit before we took over. What was used to put up before didn't cost more than $200. Who got the extra cash? The workers or the management company? So where did the extra money go? Well, these guys earned their money and we could account for every cent. The merchants were all very pleased and the Mall never looked better.

CHAPTER 14 – The Coming Holidays

Thanksgiving was just around the corner and already Patti and Debbie both wanted to cook, but Debbie won. Ed was invited to have dinner with us and spend the day watching football. He accepted but asked if he could bring a dear friend who had nowhere to go. Debbie scolded him for asking, telling him that this was his home and of course he could bring a friend. Both girls were convinced that he was bringing a girlfriend. Big Ed never talked about his friends, only his poker club guys. Randy found out that he was bringing Sid Rosen, his friend from grade school. Sid passed the bar and became a lawyer and they became even closer friends because Sid handled all Ed's legal work. That revelation threw cold water on the girls and their theory. We were all busily getting the store ready for the holiday season. The girls were placing the new merchandise around the store; they bought some glittery fabric, some flowers, etc., to decorate the shelves in the middle of the store. It was beginning to look a lot like Christmas at our store and the entire mall. We tried to group articles together to make it easier for the shopper. Bathroom items were followed by kitchen items and so on down the center aisle. Garden supplies were placed against the wall along with toys and mechanical items. Candles were scattered all over the store and the aroma was so refreshing compared to the stench of oil and hardware items. Our two windows were draped in white metallic cloth; one window was laced with bathroom and kitchen items. The other window was fixed up with mechanical and plush toys. We were almost ready to open with our holiday sales. Excitement was running high, especially for me since a lot of the items I bought looked pretty damn good on display. Everyone went home when we closed the store except Randy and me. We stayed behind to get few things straightened out for Friday. We didn't want to come in on Thursday, Thanksgiving Day. So we told everyone to go home, we would take care of our special signs for Black Friday as the day after Thanksgiving is called. Randy and I were done in about twenty minutes, but then went into the back room and had some sex that we both needed and wanted, and we also christened the bed. Andy was right. It is better to get fucked lying on your back. It feels great and the cock does go in deeper. The back room was a great idea, thanks to Randy. It was good for Big Ed to take a nap during the day, if he needed it, but we knew he would never do it. But it was a better idea for Randy and me to shack up in, and I knew we would get plenty of use from it. We were both home about 6:30 pm, had some dinner, and played with the kids and with Holly and Cleo. The kids were unbelievable with the dog. All four took the two dogs for a walk twice a day. One held the leash going down the alley, and the other held the leash coming home. But all four went together and stayed together until they got home. The leashes didn't come off until they were in the fenced yard and the kids knew the dogs would be safe. They did this on their own. I thought their mothers told them what to do, but I was wrong.

Thanksgiving Day found us getting out of bed with the aroma of fresh ham being baked along with pumpkin and mince meat pies. The table was set before Debbie went to bed. The four extensions were in place and the table would seat twelve people comfortably. Debbie was cooking the turkey and the sweet potatoes along with some other side dishes. The girls agreed, Debbie would do Thanksgiving and Patti would do Christmas. Each year they would switch because we all enjoyed spending the holidays together. Even the dogs were together on those days. I can't remember them being separated too often since we brought them home. The two families were so close - it was as though we were related. I felt as if I had four children, not two, and Randy felt the same. Dinner was at 4:30 pm so we were told eat light, save room for dinner as there was always plenty of food. Big Ed came over to our house around noon and was watching some football with us. Debbie sent her kids over to watch the game at our house. They would be in her way if they stayed home. Of course the dogs were with the kids, and after a bit, all four kids went outside with the dogs and were having a ball playing with the animals. Big Ed was very relaxed at our home. He was never one to impose, even if it was his own family. He knew that he was always welcome with us and I was glad to see him so relaxed. He did express some concern about Black Friday.

Would he have enough help? He expected a big crowd of customers when we opened. I told him that we had Gladys, Hazel, Tony, Randy, me, Debbie, Patti, you and the four kids. That will be eight of us, twelve counting the four children; thirteen, if Petey shows up. We may have more help than customers. We laughed at that prospect. I told Big Ed, I think we're in fine shape. Big Ed told me that the sidewalk sale had netted the kids around $800 and he paid each of them $50 for two days work. Of course the mother's took over the money so that they wouldn't blow it foolishly. So I opened bank accounts in the amount of $200 for each of them. They don't know about the bank accounts. Let's keep it that way.

Syd Rosen arrived at 4 p.m., and joined us with a glass of wine while we watched some football. When 4:30 p.m. rolled around, the kids were called, told to brush the leaves from their clothes, wash their hands and sit around the table. Debbie and Patti had everything under control. The menu consisted of: a toss salad; baked Virginia ham with pineapple slices and cherries that the children always wanted; turkey with all the dressings; mashed sweet potatoes with melted marshmallows on top; mashed white potatoes; green beans; broccoli; cranberry relish; biscuits; homemade gravy; and of course, it wouldn't be a holiday meal without our favorite sauerkraut and kielbasa. Debbie is Polish and we would never have a special meal or holiday without Polish sausage. As usual, at the end of the meal, we all left a little room for some more sauerkraut and kielbasa. Dessert was homemade apple pie, mincemeat pie and pumpkin pie. Patti was the expert pie maker and this was her department. As was her specialty, cranberry relish. When we finished the dinner, the children wanted to go out and play with the dogs, which I thought was a great idea to work off some of the food they had just eaten. They ran out with the dogs and the girls were clearing the table when Big Ed said,

"When you gals get done, join us at the table; I have some things I want to talk about." I figured it was about Black Friday and some concerns he may have about the business. When they joined us, Big Ed was very serious and began by saying,

"You all know how I feel about Del, Patti and the kids. I feel as though they are my own flesh and blood. I have already opened bank accounts for each of the four children in the amount of $200 each. They don't know about this and I really would like to keep it a secret for a while. The other thing is I am really proud of the way Del has taken an interest in the shop and was really proud of Randy and Del when they went to the craft shows and did a hell of a good job buying items for the store. I'm looking forward to one hell of a holiday season this year. They bought some things that I wouldn't have, but that's young blood and their ideas. Now that I look back at their purchases, I'm really pleased that they had the foresight to look ahead and buy what I would not even given a second thought to. Well-done boys! Now this leads me into another decision. I'm not getting any younger and my health isn't the greatest. With the history of my heart, I could leave this planet at any time. Randy is my heir. Everything I own is in his name. I have done this so that when I die, the government can't come in a claim anything because I don't own anything. Thanks to Syd, everything has been taken care of legally. I have also decided that the hardware shop will be given to Randy and Del. And it is in their names as I speak.

My mouth dropped open and I said "What?" Patti covered her mouth with her hands, I shot a quick glance to Randy and he gave me a quick wink and a smirk.

"That shop couldn't be in better hands than with my two sons. I've considered you as my son for quite some time now, and Del, you are my son. Why wait until I die? Settle this while I'm alive. Del, I'd like you to quit the real estate business, and take over as co-owner of the hardware shop with Randy. I know that you have been in real estate for a few years, but I'm prepared to make it worth your while to quit."

Patti whispered, "Oh my God" and began to well up. But she did control the tears. I was numb...couldn't believe my ears. Big Ed just kept rolling along.

"How much notice do you have to give them? One week is sufficient; two is customary. How do you feel?"

"I feel numb right now" and they all laughed. "Are you sure you want to do this?"

"Are you interested?" continued Big Ed.

"My God, yes. I've dreamed of something like this but never thought it would happen."

"Good, then I'm sure. I'm glad this is working out for you. I'm not kidding, Del, you're a fine young man and I am more than pleased to call you my son and your family is my family. Now, Randy and Del, there are a few things to be said. As long as I'm alive, and in control of all my faculties, I will be in charge of the store. I will sign all checks, make major decisions for the store; although you two haven't done too badly here of late. Everything will come through me. Any questions?"

"No sir!" said Randy, and I echoed the same.

"Good, Syd already has the papers drawn up and will be certified tomorrow, and he has some papers for both of you to sign. In the meantime, get that letter of resignation together and in the mail. Now, let's celebrate" and he put a bottle of champagne on the table. It was Eiffel Tower Vintage champagne.

Syd clanked a spoon on his glass and said that he would like to say something. "When Ed approached me about this transfer, I thought he was losing it. I had some serious doubts until I met you Del, and now that I have met you and your family, and have gotten to know you better, I have this to say; Ed, I have to agree with you. You have made a good choice. I have checked Del's background and find him to be a perfect person for your choice. This man doesn't have, nor did he ever have, a blemish on his record. Not many people can make that claim. His references are above reproach. Congratulations Del!"

I thanked him as humbly as I could. This was quite an honor. Randy told me later that the champagne costs about $75 to $80 a bottle, and Big Ed had purchased two bottles. So we all drank champagne and drank and drank until it was all gone. This is a Thanksgiving that I will never, ever forget. Big Ed and Syd left to meet some buddies and play poker, I had a chance to talk to Randy and learned that he has told his father that I would like to buy into the business and become a partner, after Big Ed passes. After his father had given this some serious thought for a few weeks, he made up his mind about me and ran this idea by Randy and they both approved of it weeks ago.

"And you never gave me a clue?"
Randy said, "Why should I? The look on your face was priceless. I should have had a camera for that moment. I know you were surprised. Are you pleased?"

"You know I am" as I squeezed his knee. "Now, I have to write a letter of resignation to my big boss and give him two weeks' notice."

"Don't you contribute to your retirement?"

"Yes I do. I have some money coming and I'll get it."

"If you have any trouble, don't forget Syd, he's our family lawyer and now he's your family lawyer. Don't be afraid to call on him."

The girls were chattering excitedly and every so often, they would laugh, Ed doesn't know it, but the girls are going to decorate the store. That store may never be the same.

"By the way Randy, I went to see Dr. Izzy yesterday and he tested me; I'm free of sperm. I never have to use a condom again."

"I told you it was painless didn't I?" Randy then suggested that he and I go to the store for a last minute checkup, but I reluctantly declined because my gut feeling told me no, don't go. If we went down there, we'd make love and as much as I wanted to be alone with Randy, we might have a problem when we got home and the wives would want to make whoopee, so we agreed not to go. It was so hard to say no; but I did however manage to squeeze his ass before we went home. And I was so right on target, when we got home, the kids went to bed and Patti and I made wild love because of the good news. (Pay attention to your gut feelings.) But my heart was really with Randy that night. I wanted to be with him, to hold him, kiss him, to love him and make love with him, but...!

I made up my mind that I had to talk to a doctor about my feelings for my wife, family and Randy... it just doesn't feel normal. How can I continue to have such strong feelings for both? And I know that Randy is struggling the same way I am. There's got to be an answer, a solution. I need to know. Maybe Randy and I could go see a shrink together. If not I'll go alone, but I want him to go with me. I can't believe what has happened today. I'm co-owner of the hardware store. I have to ask Randy if Big Ed is aware of our relationship. There is so much I have to do. My mind was working overtime, loaded with all kinds of questions, and they were running over and over in my mind. I thought I wouldn't get much rest tonight, but I finally did fall asleep.

CHAPTER 15 - Black Friday

Black Friday finally arrived. We all had a hard time eating some breakfast due to the anxiety of what was ahead.

When we all got there, we saw people milling around the mall. Once we opened the doors, people came in and the sales began. Gladys and Hazel were at cash registers facing each other near the entrance door. The rest of us were around the store to be of assistance to whoever needed help. The kids were to be gofers when needed. Within minutes, we were all busy helping customers get their selections. Such comments as: "I never knew that I could find this in this store; you have such beautiful gifts items;" or, " your gift selections are better than what I could find in a department store"...and so it went. Debbie, Patti and Tony were selling, bagging and answering questions, as were Big Ed, Randy and me. It was interesting to see what people were buying. It gave us a clue what to buy more of next year. The morning flew by, and not only were we busy, but we found out later the entire strip mall was very busy... a very good sign. Andy claimed that the Christmas decorations were drawing new people to the mall. He may be right; we certainly had a good crowd of people for Black Friday. We had a bit of a breather around lunchtime, so Randy called The Lounge and ordered some pizzas and Tony went down to get them. When he returned, he mentioned that The Lounge was really crowded. This was unusual because only neighborhood people knew of The Lounge. Then Tony added that he saw two nice size

signs, one at each end of the mall that read, 'HUNGRY???
Visit Angie's Lounge around back'. When we saw Andy, we
inquired about the signs and he said that he felt sorry for
Angie and Tony Serio because they were out of the way and
off the beaten path. He had signs made and put around
hoping the signs would help them out. Andy really is a
good-hearted person. We ate when we could between
customers and the crowd of people continued the remainder
of the afternoon. As business slowed, we sent Debbie and
Patti home. We told the kids to go home too, but they
wanted to stay. They were having too much fun to go home,
so they stayed. About 7 p.m., we chased big Ed home too.
That left us with two cashiers. Tony, Randy and I were
plenty of help. At 7:30 p.m. we sent the cashiers, Tony and
the kids home. We were closing at 8 p.m. and could handle
the store until then. Once closed, we pulled the shade down,
pulled the cash and put it in the safe in the back room, gave a
few kisses to each other, and wound up on the bed making
mad love. When finished, I asked Randy if we were guilty of
incest. "After all, we are legally brothers. Isn't what we do
incest?"

"Yes it is he replied and I don't intend to worry about
it. I don't intend to spread it all over town, do you?"

No, I replied, then he began to hurry me to get
dressed. We had to hurry because Big Ed said he would wait
for us at The Lounge. Randy and I got into The Lounge
around 8:20 pm and the place was crowded. We saw Big Ed
and Andy sitting on a sofa near the artificial window and we
joined them.

"Andy", I said, "Your signs worked. Look at this
place." He agreed.

"How was your business today? "

"It was fine. I think we really put a dent in our
merchandise. People are buying toys and Christmas gifts."

Big Ed said that we have got to restock in several
areas. We'll do that tomorrow. He was very pleased with
the crowd coming to buy - people he never saw before.

Andy thanked the guys who decorated when he saw them; they were the ones who did this. We all had another drink and then headed for home. It had been a good, pleasant and profitable day.

Saturday morning came around too fast. We had a quick breakfast and I couldn't get my mind off of Randy. I wanted to hold him in my arms, lick his ear, smother him with kisses, smell his manly aroma, and start all over again. I really love this man. It was pure hell to walk into the shop, see him with his dad and knowing how I felt about him but could not do or say anything but, "Good morning Big Ed, Randy." By 8:45 a.m. everyone was there and ready for the crowd. We had a few people come in right away and browse around the store looking everything over; but when they bought, it was worthwhile. The bathroom sets and kitchen sets were a big hit. We have catalogues for both items and surprisingly we had several orders for items in the catalogue that we didn't have. We promised a week to two-week delivery, which was fine. People wanted them for Christmas gifts. Randy sent our wives and children home at 2 p.m. We weren't too busy. At 3 p.m., he sent Gladys, Hazel and Tony home. We could handle the flow as it had decreased. A few people strolled in to look around; we could handle them. By 5 p.m., Randy told Big Ed to go home, we're not that busy and you have had two busy days. Surprisingly, he agreed to leave, almost eager to go.

"Got a heavy date, dad?" asked Randy.

"You know that I'm not involved with any women, but I do have an important appointment this evening. I'll leave the store in your good hands. Don't work too late. Close up early. See ya." And he left the store.

"You think he has a date?" I asked.

"Not with a woman. He doesn't have any ladies in his life. I used to think he visited a hooker for his sex life, but after being with him, no, no that will never happen. He always said that he never paid for sex in his life and he's not about to start now. And I know my dad. He's bullheaded, if he says no, he means NO."

"Randy, he's got to have some sexual release somehow. Look at him. He's a fine looking man, well built, how old is he?" "Sixty three, I think, maybe sixty four," said Randy.

"See, he's in his prime and I'm sure he has a sexual outlet."

"You may be right Del, he may have something going, but I'll bet my life he doesn't have a woman in his life. Let's close and hit The Lounge for a drink, after we play around."

"Hurry...hurry, let's hurry..." I kidded Randy. Randy and I counted the day's receipts, made out the bank deposit and closed the store as we headed for the night bank deposit located in the food store window. We entered The Lounge just as Andy was finishing his drink.

"Sorry I don't have time for a drink with you two 'Girls' but I have an appointment and I don't want to miss it. See you all on Monday. "Bye-bye" and he was out of there in a flash. We had a drink, or two or three and then headed home. On our way home, I told him of my feelings and that I felt we both needed some professional advice. He listened to me. He listened to how I felt and why I felt the way I did. I understood my strong desire to be with him more and more.

"Christ Del, you are telling me how you feel and why and it's a carbon copy of what I'm going through." He stopped the car, grabbed me and plummet me with kisses. I made him stop only because people who might know us could see us. But after very little discussion, he agreed with me; we should seek the advice of a professional doctor, a shrink. Randy and I proceeded home and as we passed Big Ed's condo, we thought we saw Andy's car parked nearby. We dismissed it, thinking that it was a car that looked like Andy's. We again agreed to see if Dr. Izzy could refer us to a good doctor.

"Speaking of doctors", added Randy, "Debbie made an appointment to have both dogs spayed next week. They go in at 9 a.m. on Monday and can come home at noontime. She was supposed to tell Patti and I was supposed to tell you but in the excitement of Black Friday, I forgot."

"Patti did mention something about the dogs but I forgot what it was."

"Well, if Debbie gives you hell for not telling Patti, blame me. It's my fault. I forgot to tell you. When you're around me Del, I have other things on my mind. I would like to go shopping tomorrow and buy some work clothes. Wanna' go?" asked Randy.

"Tomorrow? Tomorrow is Sunday, nothing open tomorrow." I replied.

"Hamilton Mall is open every day, including Sundays."

"Oh Christ, I forgot about the Mall; Okay, count me in. I could use some work clothes too. What time would you want to go?" Randy replied that he would go after lunch.

True to his word, Randy was at my back door a little after 1 pm. We went into several stores looking for work clothes. I came to the conclusion that I did not like blue denim jeans but I did find some bone colored jeans that I really liked. I had a hard time convincing Randy that he didn't like blue denim either. We were walking out of the store with each of us buying three pair of bone colored jeans, three plaid shirts each and on our way out, we saw loafers with thick rubber soles. We each bought a pair. We looked at the time and it was 3:30 pm, much too early to go home. We remembered that Andy lives near here and his building has a piano bar on the ground floor. We parked the car and as we entered the piano bar, we heard someone call our names.

"Randy, Del, over here." In the corner booth sat Andy with one of the most beautiful woman I have ever seen. She had flame red hair and it was styled to frame her face, almost a halo effect. Her complexion was flawless and her make-up was impeccable. She wore diamond earrings with a matching brooch. The soft satin powder blue dress shouted 'expensive'. This lady oozed class without any effort. Andy introduced us to Micki Martin, owner of the Martin Modeling Agency located in the Mall, New York and Los Angles. Andy invited us to join them and he ordered drinks for everyone.

"I'm glad you two came in when you did. Micki is interested in one of your employees," said Andy talking to both of us. "She has seen Tony in the Mall and been watching him, but needs some information about him,"

Micki added… "I have seen him at the Mall several times." Her voice was soft and almost sultry and her diction was perfect. I could really fall for a woman like her and I noticed she was single; no wedding rings, but a huge diamond on her right hand. She continued, "I'd like to know a bit more about him. Andy tells me that he works for you?"

"Part time," added Randy. "His name is Tony Adams. He's a college sophomore and he comes from an average family. They are not wealthy, that's why he's working part time to help supplement his college bills. He is a very clean cut kid, honest, hard worker and very, very trustworthy and dependable. What can I do to help you?" She reaches her well-manicured hands in a small purse that she has and withdraws a card, handing it to Randy.

"Give this to him and have him call me. I'll set up an appointment, interview and see if I can place him. He has a contagious smile and he seems to have perfect teeth. I'm sure that I can get him employed earning more money than he is making working part time. No offense intended to you or your store, but I warn you, you may lose an employee."

Randy replied, "I would never stand in Tony's way to make a better life for himself; he's too nice a guy for that."

She rose putting a shawl over her shoulders and said, "I really must run. I have a full schedule today. It's been a pleasure meeting you both. I often shop the strip malls; you never know what you're going to find. Look at Tony…

Thank you so much for your time. Andy, I'll call you for lunch one day soon... Toot-a loo." As she walked towards the door, several heads turned to watch that million dollar wiggle leave the bar.

"Holy shit Andy," Randy exclaimed. "Where did you meet her? Where did she come from? How long have you known her?"

"Too bad you're both married and love your wives," Andy gloated. "That's a hot piece of ass, and judging by the way she was sizing you both up, both of you could have her. Far as I know, she's single and has no boyfriend. I have known Micki for several years, and now that you mention it, I don't remember how or when I met her. I know that I have sent both men, and women to her modeling agency. Some made it, some didn't. If she does place them, I usually get a $200 check from her. I've complained that she doesn't have to send me money but she still does it. She's always been a sweetheart to me.

"How can you keep something that beautiful a secret?"
complained Randy.

"Look you two, I think the world of both of you," Andy said disgustedly," but you have to learn how the other half live. You see a beautiful woman, like Micki, and you're both gaga over her. To you, she a good-looking broad that you would both like to fuck, right?"

"Well, maybe after we got to know her better." Randy confessed rather sheepishly.

"Bullshit," snapped Andy. "You both drooled over her and would like to throw her in bed and fuck her bones. You see guys, gay men do not react the way you do. A good-looking dame is a good-looking dame, nothing more. We look at her clothes, hairdo, makeup and jewelry, like her diamonds, gold and so forth. It ends there. We are not interested in her sexually or beyond that point. That's where we differ. Now let a good-looking man come in, and every gay man in the room will turn to look at him. They will notice his clothes, his crotch, whether or not he is wearing a wedding band and the wedding band is not important, and if he's cute, they fantasize about getting him into bed, or how they can score with him. Gay men will send him a drink, strike up a conversation with him and try like hell to leave with him. The wedding band doesn't mean a thing. You two… when you walk into a room, all the gay men are cruising you, until they see your wedding bands, and that won't stop them. I told you most of my tricks are married men, so you're both fair game."

I had to laugh, "I never thought of myself as fair game, although I have become a 'crotch watcher' to use your term."

"And what have you learned?" inquired Andy

"Well, I can spot men who are wearing briefs, and I think I can tell if they're wearing boxer shorts or no underwear at all."

"Now, isn't that better than looking wishfully at good looking women?"

"Well, I still like seeing beautiful women," I replied.

"Me too," added Randy. "Don't men ever catch on that they are being watched"?

"Sometimes they do, and sometimes we pick up a trick that way, but that doesn't happen very often. If the man is a hot looking number, we make it obvious that we're staring at his crotch. More often than not, we will have a trick. Some straight men are looking for a quick fix, others haven't got a clue. I'll tell you what we gay men do. We watch movies and see the men movie stars and often times they are showing a big box or they are so strapped in, you can't see anything. TV shows are really good to watch. You can see so much more. It's wonderful to see a hunk wearing swim trunks made of spandex. You can usually see so much more. Then there are the old cowboy movies. Those movies were made before briefs were invented. Those boys are either wearing boxer shorts or nothing at all. The way some of them are hung, I'd say they are wearing nothing at all.

Now you know how most of the gay men think and live. We really have no interest in women. That's your lesson for today."

"Thanks Andy for your info. It's been enlightening," said Randy.

"Tell me guys," asked Andy, "Have either one of you ever had a real blowjob? I don't mean a quickie in an alley or some public restroom. I mean a real blowjob that makes you want to see your cocksucker again, and again."

"What's the difference?" I asked?

Well, the difference is you've got to be in bed, on a sofa or soft rug. When you're stripped down, your gay friend will begin to lick your shaft up and down. This is what I do to my tricks and they keep coming back. Then I let my tongue go around the head of their dick. They are getting hard, then I do the shaft again and this time I let my tongue softly massage the balls, very gently, then it's up and down the shaft again, around the head, again and again. All this time they're getting harder and harder. Now I'm in complete control. I slowly envelope their whole, hard dick in my mouth, and I can tell that they are tingling and really want me to blow them so that they can cum. But I like to tease for a bit longer until I feel their cock stiffen and know that they are about to climax full force. At that point, I swallow their whole cock as much as I can and I begin to speed up my motion to make them cum. Then they shoot their load. While this is happening, I'm running my tongue around the head of their dick and the sensation is almost unbearable. They are tingling, writhing their body and begging me to stop, which I do. At this point, their toenails are fluttering like venetian blinds. That my boy is how you know you've had a damn, good blowjob. Not a one or two minute quickie that some queens call a blowjob."

"Andy, is that how you give a blowjob" I asked?

"It is, and anyone that I ever gave a blowjob to will verify my statement and will admit that they come back for seconds, and when either of you want a blowjob like I just described, call me. I'm available for you two anytime."

I didn't want to let on that his description bothered me, but I was beginning to get an erection, so I crossed my legs. Randy ordered more drinks for us and said that we have to leave after we finish our drinks.

"It's almost 5 p.m.," Andy said, "I needed your company today. I have had a shocker today and your company has helped me."

"What happened, Andy?" inquired Randy,

"Well, I have been watching this movie actor for at least three or four years. He's a hunk that I would die for. He's married, has two children and he has been the apple of my eye ever since I first saw him. I have fantasized about him for years. Some of my tricks were not that hot, so I thought of him and really gave a good blowjob to my trick. I saw one of the rag sheets in the Mall last night and there was an expose on him. It seems that a reporter went into a gay bar in Hollywood and saw my hunk fooling around with another guy. When they left, they got into my hunk's car and were making mad love. Now my hunk's been outed, and everyone will know that he plays both sides of the fence. I'm so upset. Why couldn't it have been me that he picked up? I'd have made him happy. Oh well, don't mind me, I'll get over it.

On the ride home, Randy and I discussed Andy's description of a blowjob and his broken heart over his Hollywood heartthrob. We laughed at the seriousness of his statements.

"Randy, do you remember when I gave you a blowjob similar to what Andy described?"

"Yeah, I remember," replied Randy.

"Well," I continued, "Did your toenails flutter like venetian blinds?"

"No, they didn't, Randy laughed, "but they were quivering."

As he laughed, I said,

"Oh you smart ass" as I hit him on the arm, and we both laughed. When we got home, Randy called to tell me that he received a phone message call from Dr. Izzy. He has recommended Dr. Vernon Lenhart who is specialist on sexual orientation (gender identity).

"I'll try to get an evening appointment so that dad can close the store. You OK with that?"

"Sure am," I replied. "What do we tell the girls?"

"Oh, I'll think of something to cover us both. Don't worry about it," said Randy.

A few days later, we were walking into Dr. Lenhart's office. Randy told our wives that Frenchy's boss had some showcases that were in good shape and offered them to Randy for a really good price before he sold them elsewhere. We were going down to his warehouse and check them out. Little white lies. Randy also told me that he gave Tony the card from Micki and advised him to call her.

"What do you have to lose," Randy added; "something good might come from it?"

Dr. Lenhart is a specialist in sexual orientation. He told us that he normally didn't make evening appointments, but since Dr. Izzy highly recommended us, he would make an exception. And he is also seeing both of us together rather than one by one. After he made us feel at ease, he wanted to know what our problem was. Randy began by explaining that we are next-door neighbors and have been for several years. He further went on to explain that we were both married, had children, and loved our families and wives. Then Randy explained about the broken window and how we kissed each other and what's been going on since between us. Dr. Lenhart jotted down a few notes but then began to ask questions, such as "have either of you had sexual relation with anyone else, male? female? Of course the answer was no to both questions.

"Does what we have done and what we are doing make us gay?" Randy then asked?

"No, you are not gay; well you could say that you are, but… in reality, you're both bi-sexual. And here is the difference. A truly gay man will have nothing to do sexually with a woman. A truly gay man has never had sex with a woman and doesn't want to, no matter what. A gay woman, a lesbian, on the other hand, will have eyes for another woman only. Men are the least of their desires. We will not dwell with gay women today; let's just stick with the men. Gay men have eyes and desires for men only. You both have wives that you claim you both love and still have sex with them and with each other. You can have sex either way with ease. That's the difference. This is called bi-sexual. And you tell me that this has been going on for quite some time. Do you have any guilt feelings along the way, towards your wife and children, or towards each other?"

"No," we both answered.

"Well, it seems that you have the situation under control - for now."

"What do you mean 'for now'?"

"Well, it's just a matter of time, if it hasn't happened already, for someone to make a pass at you and you will follow him, or her, for some extra sexual pleasure. There are a certain group of men and women in the gay world that get pleasure out of breaking up a solid relationship just to know that they can do it. Some people are always looking for a new and different piece of tail and then once they succeed and get it, they leave you. They never intended to live with you or become a partner to you. This is how most solid relationships wind up. If this hasn't happened to either of you, thank God, and Good Luck.

Statistics prove that it just a matter of time before it will happen unless you both have iron and steel will power. Right now, it appears you both have that will power, but for how long? Right now, if I understand you correctly, no one knows about you two except you two. Most homosexuals or bisexuals adjust well to their sexual orientation. There are many men and women, more men than women, who will never settle down with one person. They are very content to pick up some one different each day or night. That's all they want to do. A different trick each day, no strings attached. They may have the same trick a few times, but they don't want to be tied down to one person. They love the carefree attitude they have to do as they please, when they please and pick up whomever they please. This is called an open relationship. However, they must overcome the wide spread social disapproval and prejudice that may follow them. This adjustment may take a long period of time and may cause some psychological stress. It's a common practice in the gay world for men and women to change partners throughout their lives. They are obviously looking for the right partner. Sometimes they find the right one, and live together, very happily for years. But many times, they do not find the one they are seeking and it's sad. Bi-sexual men, and women, play by different rules.

Let's go back to when I was a teenager. Gay people were not called gay or lesbian; they were called queer. If you were seen even talking to a queer on the street, you were branded a queer. They never heard of or used the term bisexual. The only time you could safely speak to a queer was in school. Anyway, bisexual men always married women, such as you two. You are both having sex together without the wives being aware of it. They are happy and you are both happy. You have the best of both worlds. Only God knows how many married men play behind their wives back, it is a very common practice and very widespread, and vice a versa.

Many of my male patients are married men going through what you two are going through. I have a niece who lives in Manhattan and worked for about ten years for an agency that takes movie stars and celebrities around New York when they are in town. She has always said that all the good-looking men in Manhattan are gay and they are there waiting for their big break on the Broadway stage. If and when they make good and get called to Hollywood, they continue to have sexual relations with men and will eventually marry, but continue to have their sex with men. And she's right. So many actors in Hollywood are doing just what you're doing and the beauty part is some of the wives know about it and don't care. They're doing the same thing. She has always been assigned to male actors, not women, but in talking with other employees who dote on female actors, they're not as publicized as the men. I don't know why men are more publicized. Women are just as demanding for sex as are men, yet they are not targeted. Go to a dance. How often do you see two women dancing to a slow dance? Very often and nothing is said. Let two men dance a slow dance and watch how fast they get thrown out of the club or asked to sit down. And then after all this, you have married men who have sex with other woman outside of their marriage. One patient of mine told me that he gets more sex out of the home than he does at home. His wife doesn't like sex as often as he does, so he goes where he knows he can get it. There are no statistics on this behavior.

Now if you've come here for treatment, save your money. There is no cure. The cause of homosexuality is not known any more than the cause of heterosexuality is known. There is a vast network of scientists and doctors who swear that it is in your genes. You are born this way. They cannot tell when it will surface, and it will surface, maybe when you two years old, ten years old in your early teens or in your late forties. But surface it will. And, you will have these genes, active until the day you die. There is no cure. I have had married men with a wife and children come into my office at forty-five years of age and older, complaining that they are having attractions and feelings for men. What can they do? They don't like it.

Well, the truth of the matter is there is nothing we can do for them. I have shelf upon shelf of medical books here and not one of them can give information of how to curb these desires. Oh there are preachers and some medical men, who claim that they can cure homosexual behavior, but I have never met one who has been "cured" and I've been in the business for a good many years. They claim that you made a sexual choice and they can change it. Who in their right mind would make a choice to become 'gay' today with all the roadblocks tossed in your path? As a gay couple, you are not given what you're entitled to. You pay double health insurance, need a lawyer to get you papers to visit and make decisions in hospitals for your loved one or partner. And the list goes on and on. In all my years of practice, I never met anyone who woke up and said "I'm gonna' be gay from today on"; nor have I ever met or heard of a gay person being cured of being gay or lesbian.

I'm not saying they don't exist; it's just that I have never heard of or met anyone who has. My advice to you is save your money, there is no known cure. Look at your school system in this country. Young kids in high school find out that they are attracted to the same sex. They keep it quiet because of what will happen if the news leaks out. If they go to a student councilor, who is not trained in sexual orientation, they are told go to a shrink and get help. That's not the answer. What choices do they have? Learn to live with it, or commit suicide. Look at your newspapers and see how many high school kids committed suicide last year.

We had four right here in this state alone. The kids have no one to turn to. These kids have to be encouraged, not ridiculed. Believe me guys; I know what I'm talking about. I'll let you in on a little secret, I'm bisexual. My wife died fifteen years ago and I was so lost. I began to plunge into my work and did a lot of research - ten, twelve, fifteen hours a day. It was a burning thirst for me to learn more knowledge on this subject. In my studies and travels, I met a young man who had come out to his minister that he was gay, and had been gay for several years. He heard the sermon that gay people can be cured. In today's climate toward gay people, he called on the minister for help. Well, the minister began curing him and after three years of treatment, he was declared cured, and was no longer gay, or

RANDY & DEL

homosexual, call it what you may. He was now a heterosexual, and hadn't had sex with a male for over three years. I talked and interviewed him several times and after about a month, I invited him to my home, where we had a few drinks followed by the best sex I ever had. So much for the publicized cure.

My genes erupted right after my wife died, fifteen years ago. That's when I met Eric, the convert and we have been together ever since that night, about fifteen years ago, so I know what I'm talking about. There is no cure. The experts claim there is, but I've yet to read or see the cure and have yet to meet anyone who has been cured. You two are doing the best you can with the hand you've been dealt. It's normal to have strong feelings for each other, living so close to each other and partners in a business. Don't worry about it unless there is a third person in the picture, and then begin to worry. But you seem to have the situation under control, no pet names, no openly touching. I only hope for your sake that it continues this way for you. The odds are against you, but you've been doing this for quite some time, so why shouldn't it continue?

My gosh guys, I've kept you here almost two hours. You said you wanted to pay cash so no bills would be sent to your homes. My fee is one hundred dollars per hour, but I'll settle for one hundred dollars, not two hundred dollars. Let's hope that everything continues as smoothly as it is now. Call me if you have any other problems. Love each other."

We drove home happy that we went to see him and hoping our love would continue without someone trying to break us up. Once home, we learned that our wives took the kids to see a vampire movie and would be home around 9:30 pm. We had second thoughts about having sex at home, so we left a note that we are at the store and would be home shortly. If we timed this right, we'd be home before them. Big Ed evidently closed the store early so we kept it closed as we went into the back room. This was my happy time, to be alone with Randy; to love him, kiss him, just being with him was enough for me. We made love and made love and made love and then I discovered that when Randy sat in a straight back chair, or any chair, he spread his legs, wide. I never realized how much that turned me on. I want to fall on my knees between his legs and give him a terrific blowjob. I did just that in the office this particular night. Randy was impressed and complained that I drained him dry. He gets the same treatment from me every time he sits that way provided I can accommodate him. He promised not to sit like that when we are in each other's home.

When we left for home, we arrived there about twenty minutes before the girls and kids got back from the movie. Naturally, Randy and I had to listen to and relive the vampire movie, how neat is was for a man to leap off a wall and turn into a wolf, or how ten men jumped off the wall and turned into wolves and fight other vampires. This was their exciting movie. They did everything but jump off some furniture to illustrate their point. They obviously enjoyed the movie.

CHAPTER 16 – Uncle Mary's

A ndy has been after us to go with him one night down to the gay bar where the guys who decorated and he spent some time. Danny was the regular bartender every night. The club was called 'Uncle Mary's'. There were life sized pictures of movie stars all over the club. It was advertised as a gay bar and grill. You could get a club sandwich, soup, hamburger and fries there in the food line. They had a bouncer at the door advising suspected straight people wanting to enter, that this is a gay establishment and that you are welcome to come in as long as you know that it's a gay bar. At least they knew before they entered that it was a gay bar. Some straights came in, some refused, but the place always had a nice friendly crowd. When they were really busy with a big crowd, Joey was called in to help Danny behind the bar. I wanted to go, but Randy wasn't too keen on the idea. I put it in the back of my mind and planned to work on Randy until he agreed to go. We could bring our wives according to Andy, but Randy and I both nixed that idea until we saw the place and felt the girls would feel comfortable there. I asked Andy why they chose the name, 'Uncle Mary's' for a gay bar? He replied that the owners felt all the gays would know it was a gay bar. Straight people would be intrigued by the name and show up to check it out. Most straight people, when they found out it was a gay bar, stayed and had a good time. The drinks were reasonable and the food was good. That alone brought people back; plus it was a fun bar. Danny said that the owners were thinking about having a small drag show on Saturday and Sunday nights but haven't made up their minds yet. Randy and I told our wives about the bar and that we wanted to check it out before we took them there. They were agreeable and suggested that they fit us both with chastity belts before they let us go there alone. We all had a good laugh over the belts. When we saw Andy at work, we agreed to meet him at the Lounge after work, but it was a slow day for all of us so Andy came over to our store for a cup of coffee. At that time we told him of our plans to come down to the club one night when he would be there. He was ecstatic that we would come down.

"One thing I have to warn you about," he said, "When you go to the rest rooms, go together."

"Why"? I asked.

"Do either of you virgins know what a glory hole is?"

"No, I don't" answered Randy.

"Me either" I replied. Andy sighed,

"I love you both, but you're both dumb as shit. When you go into a restroom, anywhere, not only a gay bar, you have a trough to piss in plus some stalls or crappers. If you go into a stall, you will notice a hole in the wall near the paper holder. This is called a glory hole."

"Why do they call it a glory hole?" I asked, and Andy said

"How the fuck do I know? It's always been called a glory hole, ever since I could walk. Maybe it's because when a dick is shoved into the hole, the guy on the other side sees glory that he got a dick that he can suck. I don't know. My point is, unless you want to get a blowjob from a stranger, keep your dick out of that hole." I was amazed that this is another way to suck a cock.

"Do many people use the glory hole?" I asked.

"Yes, they do. In fact there is usually a line waiting to get sucked off; depending on the time of day or night. Between five and six at night is the best time. Men getting off work want a quickie and pop into their favorite restroom for a blowjob." I had a hard time understanding the whole concept and I told this to Andy.

"Look love," he replied "there is something wonderful about the glory hole, you're horny, and you need to get your jollies off. You know where there is a good glory hole and casually drop in, there's no one waiting in line, you take a leak and notice that the glory hole is directly in line with your dick. You see an eye looking out at your dick, you begin to get hard after all you're there because you're horny so you move closer to the glory hole and gently put your dick into the hole. Then you feel someone fondle your dick and then you feel a warm moist tongue begin to suck you dick. This is exciting to many people. Someone who you don't know is sucking your cock and it feels so good. When you're done, you zip up your pants and go home feeling relaxed and relieved. No questions, no money, nothing... Married men are the ones who love the glory holes the most, no involvement. They love it.

Sometimes you can look at the floor and see what kind of shoes, color of pants or glance through the hole and get a look at the guy you just sucked off. Later in the store, you see the shoes and color pants or his face if you got a look at him; there he is walking with his wife and two small children. As I said, married men love this system. It really is thrilling to know that you can have instant sex with no questions, no fuss, no frills and no bills to pay. And in most cases, there is no recognition. It could be your cousin, your brother, uncle or even your father. It could even be your worse enemy, your best friend, your next-door neighbor or a visiting movie star who wants to suck a few dicks before show time. And you would never know who it was. Isn't this exciting? So keep your dicks out of those holes. You want a blowjob, come see me." We laughed at his humor.

But Andy said, "Seriously guys, you two are head turners. Gay and straight men cruise you when you come into a room. Both are handsome and packing a big crotch. I'm surprised that someone hasn't made a pass at either or both of you. Anybody reach out and grab your crotch or your ass"?

"No… Not yet," said Randy. I began to blush a little but said nothing.

"What's a good night to come down to the bar?"

"Friday, Saturday or Sunday's are fun nights but I guess Friday night is probably the best night."

"When are you there? I want you to be there when we come down," I told Andy.

"Whenever I have nothing else to do, I'm there. And if I knew when you're coming down, I'll be there with the guys. We should have a ball".

"We'll let you know," chimed in Randy. Andy went back to work and we relived his conversation laughing at his expressions. We agree that we would go down with Andy on a Friday night. I then asked Randy when he was going to be fitted for his chastity belt. He laughed and swatted me on the arm saying the same time you are fitted. We'll be twins that night. I just feel so relaxed and secure with Randy. It's hard for me to keep my hands off him. It's bad enough that I watch every move he makes - the way he walks, talks and smiles… I never get enough of him. So far, so good - no jealousy has entered my mind. He must have felt me watching him. He turned, smiled and gave me his famous wink and silently mouthed "I love you." There go those damn flamingos in my stomach again. Oh Happy Day.

Friday night at 7:30 p.m. found us riding with Andy to the infamous gay bar, Uncle Mary's. The place was somewhat crowded, but there was plenty of room to sit around. Andy had Danny keep a booth near the end of the bar for him. The booth held six so we had plenty of room. Our booth was adjacent to a small, I mean small, dance floor. I think it was too early for anyone to dance. Frenchy came in, and shortly after Lou came in. Joey was already there working the bar with Danny. So the whole decorating crew was there in and around our booth.

Frenchy stood by the booth and said, "Looking for us? Hi guys...Did Queen Mother whack your weenies to make you come here?"

Andy hissed, "Shut your fucking mouth and sit your ass down." Lou was laughing so hard as he sat down in our booth. "It never ends with these two," laughed Lou.

Frenchy became serious and said, "I want you guys to meet a friend of mine. I told him to be here around 8 pm. His name is Leo and I met him a little over two weeks ago. He just moved in with me and…" Andy interrupted and said,

"You met him two weeks ago and he's moving in already? Have you lost your fucking marbles numb nuts? "

"Wait till you meet him," he is so different. Purred Frenchy, "I'm already in love with him and I think he feels the same way about me. If not, the door works both ways. He can leave the same way he came in."

Andy kept pushing, "How old is he? Where did you meet him? Does he have a job? How do you know he feels the same way about you?"

"Christ, what are you? The fucking FBI?" cried Frenchy.

"You know I always look after my sister" tossed Andy.

"How old is he?"

"He's twenty five, a nurse, works at the Turf Valley Hospital and I met her in a peep show".

"Peep Show"? exploded Andy.

"Not everybody that goes into a peep show is bad," snapped Frenchy. "You go to the peep shows. How bad are you? I wasn't too impressed with him at the peep show, but after spending some time with him, I changed my mind. He's a decent kid and I like him. I think you will too, once you meet him and get to know him."

Andy gave Frenchy a knowing look and said,

"Well, we'll see." I leaned over and asked Andy,

"What's a peep show?" Just as he was about to answer me, we heard,

"Hi Frenchy" and we turned our attention to the new voice and saw a very attractive looking young man, handsome and well-built with blue eyes and black wavy hair. Frenchy kissed the young man on the lips and gave him a tight hug.

"Guys, this is Leo, my new room-mate and partner." Frenchy then proceeded to introduce us, one by one to Leo.

"Leo, this is the crazy crowd that I run around with. All but these two," pointing to Randy and me. "We did some work for them and we're introducing them to the gay world." Leo whispered to Frenchy and Frenchy replied,

"No, they're not gay, just slumming." Everyone laughed. Another round of drinks came to our booth from someone at the bar. The bar was crowed and no one could figure who sent the drinks. Andy spoke and said,

"Don't worry about it, drink and have fun. Danny or Joey will tell me." We continued to drink, carry on as only gay people can. Then we met Lulu. She was a handsome woman with beautiful yellow hair; nice figure and big boobs. Everyone knew Lulu judging from all the guys who called to her and kissed her. She spotted Andy and joined our booth. Andy had to introduce her to Randy and me. She looked us over from head to foot and said,

"You new in town? I don't remember seeing you here before." Andy then interrupted and explained who we were and about the mall.

"I heard about that mall. I have got to get out there one night and see it all lit up. I heard it looks great. Gotta' go loves, I'll be back a bit later." And she waltzed to another group of people.

"What do you think of her?" asked Andy.

"She is very personable, built nice and very attractive," answered Randy. Andy laughed…

"Take a sip of your drinks" he told us, "Her name is not Lulu, its Albert and he has the hots for our bartender, Danny, He does drag here on occasion. Every now and then, he'll come in here in drag with a new wig, or new dress, sometimes we think he does it to have some fun with the guys. Everyone loves her... except Danny. He doesn't want to get tied down and Lulu would tie him down."

"Where is the men's room Andy?"

"The end of the bar make a left, you can't miss it." Thanks I said and headed for the men's room. I found it with no difficulty but the mob of people around the bar made the trip to the restroom a bit hectic. Someone playfully grabbed my ass, gave it a playful squeeze and a soft love pat. The rest room was a clean, nice sized room, with much activity going on. The corner stall was closed and you see four feet in there. Someone was getting fucked or sucked. And at the urinal, such cruising and feeling up had to be seen to believe it. I know I was being watched. I washed my hands and left quickly. Walking back to our booth, I noticed that the bar was more crowded than before and you had to snake your way through the crowd. As I was half way back to our booth, someone gently but firmly grabbed my dick and gave it a squeeze or two.

"Hi cutie" said a pleasant looking man of about forty to forty five years old, standing by my side. "Want to have some fun?" he asked.

"I am having some fun, with my lover at the booth there." As I nodded with my head towards our booth and I continued walking towards the booth.

"Change your mind, I'm at the bar," he said.

When I got back to our booth, the crowds were festive and were having a good time, and I joined them. Then Lulu came back to our crowd and said that since Randy and I were new to the gay bar, she would sing a song for us. Andy smiled and said,

"See how you affect people? I have known that bitch for almost six years; she never sang a song for me, growled Andy."

"I guess you know who rates, huh," laughed Randy. Danny, the bartender has a hand mike behind the bar, so he asked for quiet, got it and then announced that Lulu was about to sing.   When the disco had the music ready, she began to sing. She or he had a beautiful voice that could be either female or male. When she started to sing, the crowd got quiet and you could almost hear a pin drop. And she sang...

"Get ready boys, Lulu's back in town... Don't fuck with Lulu when she's in town, she can always, always put you down..."

She brought the house down and the crowd whistled, applauded, threw bills on the floor, mostly ones but there were some fives, a couple tens and one twenty that I could see. No coins. I understand that it is a silent law that forbids coins to be tossed on the floor. Gay people don't do it. Andy had a few men who he knew, come up and whisper in his ear and he shook his head no and whispered in their ears. About 11:00 pm, Randy decided that we should go home. We had to work the next day and we had a lot of re-stocking to do. Andy agreed that it was a fun night but time to go home. While riding home, Andy said,

"I told you two that all you have to do is walk into a gay bar and the whole place goes crazy; I had several guys come up to me and want to know if you were gay and if not, did you play? I told them no, and they were disappointed."
I asked what they meant by 'do we play'?

"They wanted to know if you were straight looking for a blowjob or wanted to fuck someone. I told them NO to all the questions."

"See what I mean about you guys?" quipped Andy. "You guys come into a gay bar and you stand out like a sore thumb. Everyone is interested in your bodies. Did you enjoy yourselves tonight?" We both replied that we did. Then, I asked Andy again, "What is a peep show?"

"Oh yeah! I was going tell you when Lulu came in. Remember what a glory hole is?"

"Yes."

"Well, a peep show is a store front that when you walk in has lots of magazines and gay papers and sex toys around. Then you walk into the back room that is dark. There are a series of little cubicle type rooms. Some have doors, some have curtains, each room has a small screen, smaller than a TV screen, about twelve to fourteen inches, that you put your face to and watch a porno movie after you insert a quarter. You don't get much for your two bits. You have to put your face down to where the small screen is and you watch the peep show of either men fucking men, or little boys, women licking women or little girls. When your quarter runs out, insert another quarter to see more film. Now, while your busy watching this dirty film, what you don't know, on your first time, is that directly under the screen is a glory hole.

Someone on the other side is watching a film too and if he is horny enough, he reaches into your stall and grabs your hardened cock. If you're receptive, he sucks your cock, and you might suck his cock... Again, you don't know who it is. The big difference here is that it will cost you a quarter each time the movie goes out. I figure it costs about $1 to $1.50 for the blowjob. The other side of this coin is that some of the cubicles have doors and some of them have curtains. If the door is closed, it means 'Do Not Disturb'. If it is open just a crack, it means visitors are welcome. The same applies to the curtain. If it is drawn tight, then don't disturb, if it is not closed tightly, visitors are welcome. That's what a peep show is. "

"I don't think I'll be going to any peep shows," I told Andy.

"They're all over town for the guys who love going to them. I have never seen a woman go into one of them, though." He dropped us off at the store and said,

"Next time come down to the bar, bring the wives. We can all have some fun and the place is open until about 2:30 a.m."

Then we all hugged and said goodnight and he drove away to the Embassy Arms where he lives.

Randy and I stopped by the mall and our store but everything was very quiet. There was nothing going on at the mall, so we got back into our car, went home and called it a night. On the way home, when we passed a dark area, I gave Randy a juicy kiss and told him how much I loved him. He was most receptive. Our legs were touching and the electric charge that was going through my leg was almost nerve wracking. I'm sure it affects Randy the same way but he is the driver. We went home and when we got there, the wives and children were all in bed asleep.

Saturday morning was brisk at the store. Many new customers came into the store and were pleasantly surprised at the type and quality of gifts we were selling for a hardware store. The sales proved that the customers like it. Tony came in later in the afternoon and said that he had gone to Philly the day before to have an interview from the Greer Agency. Since the schools were all closed for about a week due to Thanksgiving, he felt that this would be best for him and he wouldn't be cutting classes. He also wanted to talk to both Randy and me after the store closed.

"Not a problem", said Randy. Ed wanted to know what was up so we brought him up to date with our visit with Micki and the possibility that Tony might get a modeling job and leave us. Big Ed said that Tony was an asset to the store, clean cut, dependable.

"We wouldn't do anything to hold him back, if he could better himself. Hate to lose him, good boy." Customers came in shifts, we'd be busy for an hour, and then we'd have a free period. This was our afternoon, the evening didn't look much better between customers, while the children were bringing up items to be restocked; I was working on my letter of resignation to my big boss in Greenville, PA, Mr. Donald Redman. I wanted the letter to be very cordial and leave the door open in case this partnership didn't work out, then I might be able to go back to Real Estate. I planned on my last day of work for Lamont being the 13th or 14th of December. Business was slow after dinner, so we sent Big Ed and the children home at 6:30 p.m. The kids did a great job; most all the new merchandise was brought up and placed under counters where we could easily get to it. We hadn't had a customer in the store since 7 pm, so we sent the two cashiers home. They were happy to get off as they both had lots to do for the Christmas Holiday. So Randy pulled the shade down on the front door and dimmed the lights at the front part of the store. He mixed three drinks; one for each of us and then we all went into the office at the rear of the store.

"Tony, what's up?" asked Randy.

"Well," said Tony, "I want you both to promise me that what I'm going to tell you will remain with you two only - promise?" Tony was almost gray in color and you could tell that he was very, very serious and nervous. We both agreed.

"Well, I called Micki Martin as you told me to, and she made an appointment for me that wouldn't interfere with my working for you. She told me over the phone that her interview would take about two hours and for me to plan on it. When I got there, I had to fill out a couple of long forms, not an application for work as I thought. It was more of a resume of my schooling, my sports activities, my social habits, what kind of girls I have dated, and my sexual affairs, how often I shower. It took me over an hour to complete the forms."

"Christ," said Randy, "I never heard of anything like that." And I remarked that applications for a model must call for different information.

"It gets better...I think," said Tony. "Then she had me pose for some shots, her photographer was there and took all the pictures. After about two dozen poses, I had to take my clothes off and he took pictures while I was stripping. Then he turned on a red and blue light and told me take all my clothes off including my underwear. He took about ten or twelve shots of me in different positions. After he left and I was dressed, Micki told me that she was impressed with the proofs and if I could go to Philadelphia within the next two days, she would set up an appointment for me with Mr. Greer. Since school is out, I went the day before yesterday. Micki gave me round trip train fare. Well, I met Mr. Greer who is about forty five, maybe fifty years old. He interviewed me about my schooling, work aspirations, hobbies, etc. I liked him. He told me to go into the back room, remove all my clothes including shoes, socks and briefs and to put on the robe hanging there and he would be in shortly. There was a daybed back there, so when I undressed and put on the robe, I found some magazines on a table, I picked up a couple and found them all to be pornographic.

As I looked them over, I began to get aroused. Well, Mr. Greer came in, smiled at me, and gave me a contract to sign whereby I get $200 a picture to start, and the longer I'm with him, I would get increases based on how often I have pictures taken. He wants me to finish college and when they need to shoot pictures, if I can't come to them for a photo shoot, they will come to me so as not to interfere with my schooling. The money is unbelievable. It's almost too good to be true. Then he sat down with me and began to talk about my future, where I could wind up, he painted a beautiful picture, and then... then ...he kissed me. I thought, well, I may not see him anymore, I have the signed contract. And then he kissed me again, telling me how handsome I was and with that he began to give me a blowjob. I was in shock; couldn't believe this was happening to me, but it was over as fast as it began... I got dressed, his secretary gave me any papers I needed and I never saw Mr. Greer again. His secretary told me to report back to Micki Martin the next day". Randy was in total shock... I couldn't believe what I just heard.

"Christ Tony, I had no idea you'd be put through this. I'm so sorry, I never dreamed..."

"Oh but it gets better" blurted Tony, "I reported back to Micki Martin yesterday afternoon and she led me to her private suite in back of her offices. She has a very nice sized apartment in back of her offices. If need be, she can stay there if the weather is too bad for her to go home. In her apartment, she made me a drink, congratulated me on my new career as a male model and here's a drink to your new, profitable life. I was going to tell her about Mr. Greer and what he did, but before I could, she was beside me, unzipped my fly, had my dick in her hands and began sucking on me. Guys, I know a little bit about the world and some of the sex that goes on it, but both of these people floored me. What should I do? I don't want to yell fowl; I have a bonafide contract, offering good money. I already received a $200 advance. The money is good and that's what I am working for. What would you do?

"Well, I'm no expert on this subject matter, but the real issue is," said Randy, "how do you feel? Are you upset that someone you hardly know gave you a blowjob? Are you a virtuous person that will let this upset you? How do you feel?"

"Hell no, this is not upsetting me. I've had many blowjobs before; college kids are always an easy mark. Many guys and girls in college give blowjobs. I guess that I was really caught off guard by both of them being that they are professional people. I just didn't expect it. And evidently you two were not aware of what they do; you acted as surprised as I was."

"Tony, when I was in college, I had a good friend of mine who was offered a modeling job just as you were. He took it and I saw him a few years later. He is still very handsome and making big bucks. He wasn't very happy with his life style and I advised him to leave; he's a college grad. He told me that he loved the prestige and mainly the money. He couldn't make that kind of money outside the modeling field. So there you have it." Randy looked at me and said, "Reminds me of my friend Joel." I nodded.

"Well" said Tony, "I wanted to run this by you and see how you felt. Micki did tell me that anytime I wanted to come here and join her in this kind of cocktail, call and tell the receptionist that I was interested in having a cocktail with Micki, she will get the call then and we will set up a time. I guess I'll go along with their schedule and if I don't like it, I'll quit. But the money is looking real good right now. PLEASE guys, don't tell anyone about this, PLEASE!"

"You don't have to worry, Tony, we gave you our word we wouldn't repeat it, and we won't. Are you going to work for us a bit longer or are you leaving now" I asked?

"I'd like to work up until the Christmas holiday, I enjoy working with the two of you and the other people in the store. I also like the people who shop here. I'm a people person and like being with people. If that's OK with the both of you, I'll work until Christmas eve?"

"Whatever time you can give us will be appreciated," replied Randy. I locked the door as Tony left and went back into the office where I sat down to finish my drink.

"Jesus Randy... Micki Martin giving blowjobs to Tony? I can't believe that a nice looking, well-educated gal like her would do anything like that."

"Looks and education has nothing to do with it," replied Randy." Either you like your sex or you don't. She obviously loves to suck men's cocks, I wonder if Andy is aware of this? There was an article in the paper recently, that more and more women are giving oral sex in order to keep their man at home. Micki must have read the same article."

"We promised Tony not to discuss this with anyone. We can't say anything to anyone," I reminded Randy.

"And Andy said that she was sizing us up and he felt we could fuck her anytime we wanted to. Now I wonder if she was interested in getting fucked by us, or giving us a blowjob." Randy started to smile and said,

"Well Del, after looking at your big crotch or box, I'm sure she wanted to blow you... lucky you." I said that she was looking at your crotch too.

I leaned over his shoulder, gently kissed Randy's ear and whispered, "If she thinks she is going to suck my cock,

I'll have yours ready for her when she's finished with me, sweetie." He giggled and pulled me down on his lap.

"I know. It's hard to believe this about her, and the guy in Philly that Tony was sent to. They're in this together. But Tony got a contract. This was after he had a contract, not before. Joel's words are ringing true about the industry."

"This is something to think about, isn't it?" I replied. "Have you noticed that Tony wears briefs and he must be really hung for those two to make him?"

"Yes, I have noticed, "replied Randy. "And let's not make plans to find out. Cabish?" I got off his lap, made us another drink, and said, "Yes, I understand, and have no intentions to check him out." And I muttered quietly, "I have my hands full with you, you handsome hunk."

"I heard that," he said as he headed toward me. When he reached me, he grabbed me, kissed me and walked me to the bed where he pushed me onto the bed and we made mad love… again… Oh Happy Day.

The news of Tony's plans to leave saddened everyone in the store. Big Ed planned to have a farewell dinner at the Pasta Palace for him and all the employees at the store. He made arrangements for the Palace to have two tables set up; one for the four children and another right beside it for eight adults. The kids were young adults and felt very grown up to be at their own table. Gladys and Hazel suggested getting Tony some good luggage as a farewell gift. We all agreed and they bought it, all of the gang chipped in except for Big Ed. We all signed the card but Big Ed had his own card with a $100 check enclosed. Tony was on the verge of tears and he managed to say, "If this doesn't work out for me, can I come back and work for you?"

Big Ed said, "As long as I'm in that store, you will always have a job with us." Then he turned to me and said. "Did you get a resignation letter off to your big boss in Pennsylvania?"

"Yes I did," I replied. "It was mailed the other day, I requested that my last day be the 23rd of December; the same day as you Tony."

"Perfect timing, good," said Big Ed. "Now we're cooking on all burners. If they give you any trouble, let me know. I'll get Syd Rosen on them. He's your lawyer now too. Don't be afraid to call on him, he's a great guy and he will do well by us all if the need ever arises. We go way back to third grade. We have been good friends all those years, and he has been my lawyer ever since he graduated law school and passed the bar." Just then, Andy walked over and wished Tony good luck.

"Pull up a chair and join us with a drink", which Andy did. Big Ed motioned the waiter to give him what he wanted to drink and put it on our tab. It was a very nice farewell dinner for Tony who did shed a few tears. After hugs and kisses were exchanged, the party broke up. Our wives took the children home and we said we'd be home shortly; we wanted to talk to Andy for a bit. Big Ed left when the kids left, while Randy, Andy and I were still drinking at the table. We told him that Tony seems to have a good job lined up and how happy he was to get it. The money was the big draw. Randy and I did not mention anything that Tony had told us about Mr. Greer or Micki. In fact their names never came up in our conversation.

Andy said he wished he had a dime for every guy that came up to him at Uncle Mary's wanting to know more about the two hunks with him Friday night.

"Christ, I was going to have a sign made and placed on the table tell everyone that you're NOT gay. I told you. All you two have to do is walk into a bar and all heads turn... Everyone wants a piece of your ass or to suck your cock." I laughed and so did Randy.

"It will never happen," laughed Randy.

"And you" I tossed at Andy, "I never looked at a man in my life the way I do now, thanks to you and your education on jewelry, crotches and boxes. Now, every time I see a man coming into the store or walking towards me on the street, I look at their face and then my eyes drop to look at their crotch. I crotch watch as much as you do... It's amazing how old I am and never gave a thought to crotch watching until you pointed it out to me. Now I watch every guy I see and figure he either has on briefs or boxer shorts."

"Or maybe no underwear at all," added Andy.

"Or maybe no underwear at all," I echoed Andy. We all laughed at the remarks.

"I'll never forget the day you were all looking at my jewelry... dumb me," said Randy.

"Well" said Andy, "if you got it, show it. You never know what will come of it. Good night guys." And he headed for home and we followed suit.

When we're alone in the car at night, I always sit very close to Randy, and when I can, I feel his leg or gently squeeze his 'big' crotch; as Andy would describe it. I have to stop doing that because it always turns him on and he wants to stop and have sex right then and there. No can do all the time.

"Look... isn't that Andy's car? It's parked right near Big Ed's car." Randy uttered and slowed down almost to a stop and I took a good look at the car.

"Does Andy have a rainbow decal on his rear window?" I asked?

"I don't know," answered Randy.

"If it is his car, what's he doing down here?" I asked? "Well, tomorrow when we go to work, we can check his car for the decal..."

"Hell, while we're here, jot down his tag number then we'll know for sure that it is him," Randy demanded.

"Good idea," I replied as I jotted down his tag number 'BB- 1418'. Then Randy continued on our way home, puzzled over Andy and the car.

Our sales increased during the days after Thanksgiving. People were drawn to the 'White Village', as the mall was called. We saw people that never shopped with us before and they loved the decorations and most of the many items that they bought were for Christmas gifts. Several of the people from Uncle Mary's came to see the mall that they heard so much about, and many bought gift items from us. Even Lulu came in and bought some things. I did not recognize her when she came in and talked to me. She knew that I didn't recognize her so she sang a few bars of Lulu, in a very low voice. Then the dawn hit... I recognized her and the voice.

Once I knew who it was, we began chatting like two old ladies. She loved the store with so many unusual items to buy for a hardware store. She spent about $80 in the store and was going over to see if Andy could bring her packages to her. Lulu was about five feet, eight inches tall, blond crew cut, and slender. I took him to be about twenty five years old, give or take a few years. Andy told me that dear Lulu was going to be thirty nine years young. Not many people believed her. She was always showing her driver's license to prove her age. Then Andy told us that the gay people, mostly from the bar, came to check out the 'raved about decorations', and to take a good look at us in daylight and look at our crotch. Well, when I look at Randy's crotch, he is well hung and shows big. I always look at his crotch... when I'm not fondling it. And I'd rather fondle it as well as look at it. I seldom pay attention to mine, but Randy does.

Closing the store was a good time for me. Andy picked up Lulu's packages and put them in his car, and said he would drop them off at her condo. We would count the cash and receipts, make out a deposit slip for the bank, set the registers for the next day, go in the back room, make a drink and usually fool around for a spell. This was about the best time of the day for me. I think Randy liked it too, but never wanted to admit it to himself or me. Of course, when his ramrod got big and hard, he didn't have to say a word. I knew.

After Thanksgiving, time was precious to us. We had the store to manage and run, and Christmas trees and decorations to get down from the attic. Randy and I would assemble the trees for our wives and children. Then, when they had time, they could decorate the trees. We also had to get our outside decorations put up and try to get it done before the cold weather really set in to hold us back. Randy and I worked together on the outside decorations, and believe it or not, it went more smoothly than I thought. Then I had the Real Estate office to think about. Thank God that I had a good gal who could and did run the office. She told me not to worry... if she needed me, she'd call on my cell phone. She knew that I was working at the store to get ready for the holidays.

I decided then to get her an especially nice Christmas gift. While we were stringing lights outside, we talked about gifts for the wives. Randy and I couldn't get them the same things; they would really raise hell about that. Patti told me years ago that she always wanted something personal for a gift, nothing for the house. It seems that Debbie had given the same message to Randy. While working on the lights, we decided to give them a bottle of their favorite perfume along with a check to buy themselves some clothes. Few men ever satisfy their wives when it comes to buying clothes unless the wife is with you, picks out what they want and you pay for it. Both wives fully realize that with the store, we are very limited with time to go shopping. They did the shopping for the children and any other gift shopping that had to be done. We all contributed to Big Ed's gift.

We agreed to have him fitted for a new suit, sport coat, shirts, slacks and shoes. This man never buys himself anything, so the wives took over and got him some new clothes that he sorely needed. They took an old suit of his to get the right size. This way, his Christmas gifts will be a surprise. The store help, Gladys and Hazel, always receive a check for Christmas and they always enjoy money. Things were moving along better than I expected. Big Ed was VERY happy when he saw the sales receipts with all the new merchandise that was sold. We almost tripled what we spent at the craft shows and we had about three weeks to go. He was VERY happy. In the excitement of the season and sales, we forgot all about Andy's license plate and tag number. Randy took a break and ran over to his car, and while pretending to look for something in his car, he got Andy's tag number, and noticed a rainbow decal on the rear window. The tag number was BB 1418. Randy was happy, the mystery was solved. It was Andy's car. Another mystery... what was it doing over near Big Ed's condo? Randy got back to work and began waiting on some customers as soon as he entered the store. Randy and I were busy for the next few hours, then it slowed down and we had a chance to grab a bite to eat in between customers. When we did get a breather, I asked Randy about the license tag and he told me it was Andy's car.

"What are you going to do about it? He may have a friend over there, who he visits from time to time. There's probably a good reason for his car being there." I offered in defense of Andy.

"Well, you're probably right but I'm curious as to why he is there so close to us and my dad and never letting on," Randy replied.

"Maybe it's none of your business," I replied.

"You could be right, I'm just curious."

"Good luck," I said.

We were busy until we closed. Big Ed helped with the bank deposit. Andy walked with him to make the deposit. Once made, Big Ed said good night to us and he went on home, and Randy and I restocked some of the shelves for the next day. I finally got a letter from Lamont Reality signed by Mr. Donald Redman, the big honcho of the company. He expressed his regrets that I was leaving, wishing me all the success in the world. If ever I needed any references, he would be there for me. The 23rd would be fine as my last day, and he would be down to see me before I left. I announced that I would be spending more time at the hardware store until the 23rd, when I would then be there full

time. Things were working out just fine for me and my new
venture as co-owner of the hardware store. Big Ed was
thrilled that it went smoothly.

"Why wouldn't it?" Randy asked? "Del has been a
good, faithful employee. No reason for it not to go
smoothly."
Big Ed said that "sometimes companies hate to lose a good
worker and do their damnedest to block them from leaving."
Anyway, we all planned to celebrate with a drink or two at
The Lounge; which we did after closing the store.

Andy walked in and said, "I saw your cars on the lot
and figured that you were down here having a drink. So I
thought I'd join you. Big Ed ordered Andy a drink, and we
sat there telling Andy the good news about my leaving
Lamont very shortly and assuming my new role as co-owner
of the hardware shop.

The Lounge wasn't too crowded, so we had our little
corner to ourselves. Big Ed ordered more drinks, and after
finishing his, he stood saying good night. He was tired and
wanted to go home and hit the hay. We thanked him for the
drinks and he left. Randy seized the moment and began to
question Andy about his car being seen up the road at the
condos parking area, near his dad's condo. Andy turned
white "You saw my...... You saw my car there?" He
glanced around the room and when he saw that there was no
one near us, he asked Randy,

"Do you love your dad?"

"Of course I do, what kind of stupid question is that?"
Andy glanced around again and leaned forward. In a low
whisper, he said,

"Promise me you won't repeat what I'm about to tell
you." We both promised and he sighed saying, "This would
kill your dad if he found out I told you.

"Tell me what?" Snapped Randy visibly irritated.

"I've been servicing your father for over a year now",
in the same low whisper, "and he doesn't want anyone to
know about it. He would like people to think he has a couple

of girls that he services. But he doesn't. I give him blowjobs every time he calls and wants one. He especially doesn't want you two to know what he does." Randy said that he thought his dad did have a couple of girls he played around with. Never met them, but dad doesn't tell me everything.

"No he doesn't," said Andy. "He wants you two to think just what you're been thinking, that there are girls involved."

Randy asked, "Does dad just get a blowjob from you or does he return the favor?"

"No way, your dad is piece of trade, that's gay talk for one way. I do him, he just lays there until it's over, then I sometimes have a drink with him before I leave. He doesn't pay me, so don't worry about that. I like your dad. I never charged anyone in my life for a blowjob. Your dad is a perfect gentleman. I have been doing your dad for a little over a year, and his main concern is that one of you or both of you would find out and hate him for it. That's why you saw my car at the condo a couple of times."

Randy was a little pale and all I could do was squeeze his knee, my way of giving support. Randy spoke very quietly,

"My dad is my dad, and is entitled to whatever happiness he can get. Did he tell you why he preferred a blowjob as to sex with a woman?"

"Yes," replied Andy. "He hasn't met a woman he can trust as well as he did with his wife, your mother. He feels that they are all out for what they can get, and he did look but came up empty handed. He feels safe with me and believe me guys; I love him as if he were my dad. He is very safe with me, and has been, since I've been seeing him. There is no love affair here, so rest at ease on that point. I still love my marine, Dave. I just want to see a nice guy like your dad enjoy life while he's here, and if I can help, here I am. But again, PLEASE, don't let on about this. I feel terrible that you found out the way you did. I wouldn't want him to think he couldn't trust me."

"Well, to say the least, it's been one hell of a shock for me to find out what I did about my dad," said Randy. "No, I'll never let dad know about his little secret with you" and he turned to me and said, "How about you Del?" I nodded my approval, "My lips are sealed." Andy gave a sigh of relief and said

"Thank you guys, I'll love ya both till the day I die. Thank you! Thank you! We'll all act the way we always act around Big Ed. He should never know about our meeting tonight." We agreed and had another drink, which we really needed at this point.

On the ride home, I told Randy, "I told you your father had to have a sexual outlet somewhere, never dreaming it was with Andy."

"You were right... for a change," replied Randy... just before I smacked his arm.

"What do you mean for a change?" Randy laughed and said he wanted to see if I was paying attention to him. He got another smack on the arm for that crack. We stopped the car in a very dark area just long enough make up, (not that we were mad), get a juicy kiss, and then drive on home. Randy and I planned to keep this information very quiet and continue to act as if nothing had happened. Now we knew that when Big Ed left early because he had an important appointment to keep, the appointment was with Andy. Randy had a hard time realizing that his father was doing the same thing he was doing. I tried to calm him down by acting as if this was nothing to get upset over.

"Who would think that a father, a grandfather, would do such a thing?"

I shot back, "Who would think that a happily married man, father of two children would do such a thing?"

"Well, this is different, the older man should set an example."

"Well, maybe he did" I tried to explain... "And you are following in his footsteps."

"You think my dad gives or gave a blowjob?" Randy wailed.

"No, I don't….but what if he did? How bad would that be for him? You do it. Do you feel that you are an undesirable?"

"Hell no, I don't feel bad or guilty about it… no one knows and it happened to us by accident. I am not sucking anybody behind your back, and I am pretty sure that you are not sucking anybody behind my back".

"Come on Randy, get a life. Your dad has done pretty well for himself in this world, and look what he's given you."

"Don't misunderstand me, Del, I don't hate him. He's my dad and I love him, no matter what he does or has done. It's just the shock of finding out what's going on.

"Look Randy, you've learned something about your dad. Put it behind you. Don't worry about it. Act like you did before you found out. No one knows but the three of us and it will stay like that for as long as he lives. Be happy that he has found someone that he can trust and get the enjoyment out of life that makes him happy."

"How would you feel if it was your dad?"

"Well Randy, my dad died when I was six years old. I never had a father, and my mother never married again. But I would probably feel as you do right now, except, since I met you and have had a relationship with you, I feel differently. I've never been happier. And if I thought my dad was as deeply in love as I am, I wouldn't want it to ever change. More people should feel as I do about our kind of love."

"I guess you're right Del, but it isn't easy trying to act like nothing has happened."

"Randy, you'll live and think of how you or your dad would react if he found out about us?"

"Oh Christ... I never thought of that. We've got to be very, very careful, Del. I don't want anything to break us up. I mean that from the bottom of my heart. I love you too.

Probably more than I show it, but I really love you," proclaimed Randy. I never saw Randy that solemn before. We didn't talk about his father's sexy past time any more. We continued to make love for our own sexy past.

CHAPTER 17 – First Snowfall

Wwoke up to our first snowfall. It wasn't much, about four inches, but it was so cold and windy. It was a dry snow and could cause trouble if it created drifts along the road. Snow plows were out and trucks throwing rock salt. The main roads were open and school buses were predicting one hour delay. Otherwise it was business as usual. The store was warm when we got there. Big Ed got in early and turned up the heat. He waited for us to get in so that we could clean the sidewalk and get ready for business. He had the coffee pot brewing and brought some pastries from home. When the gals, Gladys and Hazel, arrived, they were glad to be indoors and watch the weather cause some havoc outside. In spite of the weather, we had customers come in and shopped as they have every other day. The weather did not seem to hold them back. Big Ed told us that this was a better day for sales than usual. The snow brought the shoppers out. The weatherman's forecast was for some snow flurries, strong winds and snowdrifts on the roads. Some ice would form on the roads as a result of drifting snow. Caution was advised when driving for the remainder of the day. We had a slight rush around dinner and it seemed that most shoppers were going home before it got dark. When it slowed down, we told the gals to go home; we would close the store since we lived so close. Big Ed got the word to go home, even though he lived very close to the store. He went without an argument and that left Randy and me to close the store later. When we had some free time, we replenished the stock from under the counters and began to get the store ready for the next day. By 7:30 p.m., we felt we had seen our last customer for the night. Randy and I closed the store before 8:00 p.m., as the entire strip mall was deserted. We felt the weather had chased the shoppers home. We made out the bank deposit and poured ourselves a drink. Randy looked very tired or worried, I don't know which, so I began to message his shoulders and back.

"What's wrong?" I asked, "You look worried about something."

"I know I shouldn't worry about my dad, but it keeps popping in my mind."

"You mean him and Andy?" I asked?

"Yeah. I know we promised not to discuss it but I can't help thinking about it."

I didn't know how to calm him down so I tried the only thing I could think of at the moment. I slid my hand down his shirt, unbuttoned a few buttons and began fondling his nipples until I had him aroused. It didn't take much to get him off the chair and on to the bed. The rest is history. I had him so hot that he didn't have time to think of anything but us. While we were nestled in each other's arms, I said we should call home and tell them we'd be getting a bite to eat at The Lounge and would be home later. Randy volunteered to call and when he hung up, told me that Patti was there with the kids, and all is well. We freshened up a bit, and headed for The Lounge to get something to eat and drink. The Lounge had a nice crowd considering the weather. Just as we were getting ready to eat, Andy came in. He had a late appointment for hair styling and just got finished. He joined us and ordered something to eat. Andy didn't feel like rushing home and preparing some food or going to a restaurant, so he came down to The Lounge for a quick snack. He again thanked us for promising not to talk about his affair with Big Ed. I could have kicked him right in his balls. Andy got one of my famous dirty looks. I just got Randy out of his funky mood and along comes Andy bringing up the sore subject again. Much to my surprise, Randy told Andy that it was no problem and he changed the subject, talking about the weather and the weather forecast for tomorrow. None of us heard any late reports about tomorrow. No one wanted any more snow. Our conversation switched to what's going on at Uncle Mary's? We never did resume discussion about Big Ed and Andy. I think Andy got the message.

CHAPTER 18 – Lamont Farewell

Lamont Realty took me out to a great dinner for my farewell party. Mr. Redman himself came in town for the dinner. I was very surprised and I might say, honored that he was there. He never attends these parties; he always sends someone to represent him. That's why I was honored and surprised to see him there. He gave the same speech that he always gives at these affairs when he attends them. At least I've heard this speech before. What a great asset I have been to the Lamont team, they're going to have a tough time replacing me, and should I find that this new venture is not what I really want, they want me back. It lasted every bit of twenty minutes. My staff was most sincere as I always treated them well.

I was given a beautiful hand tooled attaché bag from Lamont Reality, along with a plaque naming me for my years of devoted service. There were various gifts from my staff, such as a pure silk scarf, leather gloves, a traveling kit filled with toiletries and a cash gift of $200. All in all it was a pleasant evening, and I was glad when it was over. When it was over, I almost ran back to the store to Randy and my new family. I was really surprised that they didn't invite my family to the dinner, they usually do. Let's hope that I never have to return to real estate for a living.

It was good while it lasted, but my future looks much brighter as my own boss, and with my partner Randy, it looks very bright. I was really horny this night but thought against having sex with Randy. My mother always told me to respect my gut feelings when I got them. I had one right now and fought against myself, and as much as I wanted to hold Randy, kiss him and love him, I suggested that we go home. We did and my gut feeling was right. Patti wanted some sex very badly. I'm so glad that I could satisfy her and keep her happy. Listen to your gut feelings.

Coach Wilson had called and talked to Patti about the kids and their ice skating. He wanted to take them to Wilmington, Delaware where they have a championship rink that most of the international stars and beginners use. Wilson said that one must make reservation to use the rink. You can't use the rink while the professionals are practicing. He got it for the coming weekend, and he wanted Linda and Eddie to work out and get the experience of a professional rink. The mothers are invited to come along and chaperone their children.

The skating committee finds out the best hotels to stay at, and the hotels give discounted rates so that the cost won't be prohibitive. Patti asked if she could take her other son with them for the weekend. Wilson said by all means, we want the family to get used to the ice skating circuit. He further added that he is so proud of the way Linda and Eddie have taken to skating. He has aspirations of them getting to go to the U.S Winter Olympics in two years when they are in Canada. Patti said she would talk it over with her husband and also Debbie, Linda's mother. Wilson was pleased and it would save him another phone call as he has plenty to make. Wilson said,

"Let me know by Friday, if you can."

Debbie has told Randy that she wanted to take horseback riding lessons. She has always wanted to do it and now would be the perfect time. She had asked Patti to join her, but Patti refused claiming that she wasn't interested in horseback riding lessons. She had applied for a part time teaching job at the school, and was waiting to see if they would call her. So with Randy's blessings, she went and enrolled as a student with the Stiller Farms Riding Academy. She agreed to the three day per week plan - Monday,

Wednesday and Friday. She would begin training after the first of the year. When told of Debbie's decision to take riding lessons, Randy said that it was OK with him if that's what she wanted to do. It meant that she would have to buy some riding clothes and boots. Stiller Farms had a riding shop near the stables where you could buy all the equipment you would need to take riding lessons. It would mean one stop shopping instead of running all over town trying to find the clothing you wanted. Again Randy agreed and asked about insurance. Should he notify his carrier about her riding lessons? Debbie said that the Riding Academy insures all students and picks up the insurance costs in the fee for lessons. So be it.

Next was the weekend trip to Wilmington, Delaware for ice skating. When Patti explained the trip, the perks and prestige that could come from it, and trips like this one, Debbie agreed to go along. So both wives and four children were going to Wilmington, Delaware to watch the ice skating, do some sightseeing, and of course, do some shopping. I was elated to hear this wonderful good news. This meant that Randy and I would have a Friday, Saturday and Sunday all to ourselves. The only thing we had to do was care for the dogs, and that will be a piece of cake. Oh happy days... The trip wasn't planned until the middle of January and that would be here before you knew it. I wanted to grab Randy right now and kiss him, hug him, nibble on his ears, just make wild passionate love to him, and spend the night with him, but that would have to wait until another time. Believe me, the wait won't be easy. I'll have to settle for a quick feel or kiss until we can spend the night together in bed, for two whole solid nights. All Randy has to do is touch me and I get horny. Hurry up January, get here fast.

Randy and I had agreed to go back to Uncle Mary's, with our wives. Andy was thrilled when he found out and asked us to come down on a Friday night, because Lulu would be singing and the place would be crowded and a lot of fun. The wives agreed. When we got there, the place was getting crowded and Andy had reserved us a corner booth where we could see the whole bar, the floor show and most everything else. Danny was busy at the bar dressed in red shorts and a Santa Clause hat on his head… no shirts, bare chested. Joey was helping out behind the bar and he was dressed like Danny. In fact, all the male waiters were dressed like Danny and Joey. There were no female waitress's working tonight. Many of the guys came over to say hello to Randy and me. We introduced them to our wives, and they were charming to them with some small talk and holiday wishes. Lulu came over and sat with us and she too charmed the wives. They couldn't believe that Lulu was the same person that they waited on in the store. Of course, Lulu had her best gown and wig on for the show tonight. In the store she was a man, dressed as a man and looked like a man. Patti asked,

"What is your real name? I can't call you Lulu all the time."

"Why not, everyone calls me Lu or Lulu. My real name is Albert Peter Vincent; do you know what they would do to me with the name 'Peter'? They'd crucify me. Please call me Lu or Lulu. I'm used to it."

By this time the bar was really crowded, and noisy. The place was really jumping. Two very young, very shapely gals came out on the floor and began to dance and sing. Not only were they talented, but they were both beautiful and pleasing to look at. They were both partially nude from the waist up. Thin gauze like material covered their breasts, just enough to draw your attention to the fact that they had perky tits and you wanted to fondle them. When the number was over, they came out to the whistling and cheering crowd, took a bow and left the area. Debbie said that she thought they were really beautiful girls, and Patti agreed that they were very beautiful and talented. Then a stand-up comic came out and insulted people, and the crowd loved him. The two girls came back out and sang a very moving love song that seemed to reach everyone in the room, and again brought the house down. Debbie and Patti wiped the tears from their eyes and again commented on how beautiful they were. Andy said that,

"The girls would be happy to hear your remarks, but they are not girl, they are young men doing drag." Just then six young ladies came out and began singing and dancing to a Christmas song. All six were very scantily dressed, and it was obvious that they were showing off their breasts as well as their talent. As they were finishing their song and dance routine, out comes Lulu in a tight fitting red sequenced dress trimmed with white fur, very revealing to say the least. She looked stunning. They all sang, 'We wish you a Merry Christmas and a Happy New Year'. The audience went wild. The Christmas show was appreciated by the crowd. The girls or guys had money stuffed in their bras and in their hands. They made out pretty well. Patti picked up on the conversation she was having with Andy before the show continued.

"Andy, how can you expect me to believe that these girls are guys? Look at their tits, they're perfect." Andy replies that they are guys.

"In order to be a good female drag today, you must have tits that you can show and not padded bras, be a certain height and weight, plus be able to sing and dance. These six young men have all had silicone injections to get their breast looking real." Patti and Debbie were shocked.

"I don't believe it." Debbie replied, "They are beautiful and their bodies are fabulous."

"Well," said Andy, "I've been in the rest room with all of them and they use the same urinals that I do."

"Oh my God, I find this so hard to believe." claimed Debbie.

"Me too," chimed Patti. "If I didn't see it with my own eyes, I would never have believed it."

"Well, it is true, said Andy, and they get paid big bucks because of how good they look and how well they perform."

Just then the entertainers came out and began to mingle with the crowd. Andy called out to Kevin, a shapely redhead, who was one of the dancers. He came over and slid his arm around Andy's neck.

"Hi love, did you like the show?" Make no mistake about it, his voice was masculine. They kissed each other on the cheek and Andy told him how good the show was. Andy then introduced Kevin to Debbie, Patti, Randy and me. Andy explained that the ladies couldn't believe that these lovely girls were guys. Kevin slid into the booth next to Debbie and said,

"I can prove it to you if you really want to find out. I do this all the time with other women. He took her hand and before she knew what was happening, he placed her hand on his crotch. Debbie pulled hand back so fast, you'd think she was bitten by a snake.

"Oh my God Patti, he is a man." The entire table roared with laughter. He offered to take Patti's hand and she said,

"No thank you, I'll take Debbie's word for it. Are all of you girls really men?" Kevin said that they were and that they have been entertaining for the past two years as a group.

Patti asked "What happens when you don't want --- a--- tits anymore? Are you stuck with them forever?" Kevin laughed and said,

"No, the doctor that gave me these will get rid of them for me when I decide to become flat breasted again. And it will happen, but not just yet. I'm making good money right now, and while I'm able, I'll continue to sing and dance."

"But," Debbie interrupted, "how do you live every day? Are you dressed as a man, or a woman? Your long hair and your boobs, how do you hide them as a man?"

"I don't," Kevin replied. "When I go out during the day, most of the time I dress as a woman, I dance in high heels and I walk very well in high heels, and I have clothes that fit the occasion. I never had a problem yet. If I want to be dressed as a man, I wear a cap with my hair rolled up under the cap or a pony tail which a lot of men have today and a loose shirt or sweatshirt hides the boobs or tits and I go on my merry way."

Lulu appeared at the booth, and said that the management wanted them to do another number. Be back stage in five minutes. Kevin left saying I'll be back after this song and dance.

Patti said, "Well, I certainly have had an education tonight. I never thought they were men, they're so feminine and beautiful."

Debbie said, "Take it from me, I know...when I felt his privates, well, it leaves nothing to your imagination."

Randy laughed out loud and kidded, "Deb, I thought you touched an electric wire the way you pulled your hand back. I never saw you move that fast," and we all laughed.

"Had I known what he was going to do, I would have resisted," defended Deb.

Andy said, "Well now you know that they are all female impersonators, including Lulu, and they are under the age of thirty, except Lulu, she's older." Another round of drinks arrived at our booth from Danny. I had to take a leak so I excused myself and headed down past the bar to the rest room. As usual, the rest room was a bee hive of activity. All the stalls were occupied and there were men watching everyone who came in and out. I headed toward a vacant urinal and felt many eyes watching me. So I stood closer to the urinal, did my business, zipped up and went to wash my hands. As I left the room, I had someone feel my ass and murmur "very nice, baby." I kept on walking into the bar that was really crowded now. I had to snake my way back to our booth and many hands felt my ass and a few felt my crotch. But it was so crowded; you couldn't tell who was doing it.

When I reached our booth, I sat next to Randy and he looked at me and said, "Mad house, huh?" I agreed. Lulu and the girls came out and began to sing 'Silent Night' followed by 'We Wish You a Merry Christmas'. When they were done, and left the dance floor, Santa Clause came out and began wishing everyone a Merry Christmas. Then he began passing out festive key rings with Uncle Mary's name on an attached disk to the key ring. Then Lulu and the six girls, or boys, came out and helped Santa pass out the key rings. When everyone had been given a key ring, the entertainers began to mingle with the crowd. Kevin brought two girls with him and introduced us to Bruce and Kyle. Then Lulu found her way to our booth and she ordered drinks for all of us; her Christmas wish for all of us. She also had a few key rings if anyone wanted them.

She was on cloud nine. Danny, her heart throb, agreed to take her home when the club closed. She was beside herself. And I could tell that she was on cloud nine. When we decided to leave, there was much kissing and hugging going on, with our new found friends and it was apparent that everyone had a good time. The topic on our way home was about the girls that were actually young men. Patti and Debbie still could not believe that young men would have silicone injections to have tits, and then show them off to the public as dancers. In the gay world, everyone knew, but in our straight world, we found it hard to believe.

"I believe... I felt one." Debbie complained and we all laughed at her shock.

"How was it Deb, did you get a handful?" Randy teased and we laughed again.

Debbie said, "All I felt was a small pecker and two balls and that was enough for me. I am convinced that they are all men. I just can't believe it,"

I changed the subject... "Tomorrow is Christmas Eve and we should make reservations, if it's not too late, for all of us including Big Ed and the kids to go out for dinner. We could try the Embassy Suite or Pasta Palace. Which would you prefer?" Embassy Suite won with Pasta Palace next if we couldn't get into Embassy. We had agreed to close the store at 5:00 p.m. so that the employees could get with their families.

Most of the stores on our strip were doing the same thing, so we were in step. We got home about 1:00 a.m., but we all had a good time and no one complained. All four kids were at our house sleeping as Patti's mom was baby-sitting. The kids enjoyed sleeping at our house or Randy's. They often did this even if we were all home. They really were good kids. Patti and I had sex before falling into a deep sleep. Eight o'clock came too early for me, but we had to open the store at 9 a.m. So I got up, let Patti sleep and was at the store by 8:45 a.m. Big Ed was there, the store was warm and the aroma of fresh coffee filled the store. Big Ed was such a gem; I really loved him as a father. Randy came up from the basement with some stock items. He got there about 8:30 a.m.

We were ready for the shoppers. Many of our items were on sale, but not too many. Items that were slow movers were marked down. Even with the markdown, we would still make money. Randy got reservations for dinner at the Embassy Suite for nine of us at 7 p.m. We had been invited to several parties but we decided to spend New Year's with our families and Big Ed. Patti's Mom would come over and we would spend the holiday in one of our homes, probably mine, and I was glad to have it that way. The kids would enjoy being up until midnight to watch the ball fall on TV. This would be a big event for them and the two families would be together.

Business was slow at the store. We had enough business to make the day profitable, but we didn't need all the help, so the girls were sent home around 1:00 p.m., and we closed the store at 5:00 pm, and sent Big Ed home. Randy and I cleared the register, made out the bank deposit, made sure that the heat was on high enough so that the pipes wouldn't freeze, exchanged a few kisses and a few feels, longing to fuck each other but not tonight. As we left to make the bank deposit, we ran into Andy who also closed for the day.

"Where are you two going tonight?" Randy told him of our dinner plans at the Embassy. "I may eat there myself tonight, but you get some free time, come on up to my place. I'm having a few friends in, nothing fancy, just cocktails and hors D'oeuvres." Randy explained that we would be tied up all night with the two families but thanks for the invite.

"Maybe I'll see you at the Embassy, but in case I don't have a healthy, happy New Year" and he hugged us both as he headed for his car. A very light snow was beginning to fall and as cold as it has been, the snow clung to the ground and was blowing around the streets as traffic was creating a wind. We both went home, and after a quick shower and a cocktail, we headed for the Embassy. Big Ed was already there sitting at our table. After we were all seated, drinks were ordered and the children had Shirley Temples; they felt so adult with them.

Big Ed said, "Randy, Del, I want you both to know how pleased I am with both of you, my two sons." Just then Syd Rosen arrived and joined us at our table. Big Ed invited him to join us since he has no family in the immediate area. "I was just telling my sons what a great job they did with the Christmas sales. I was a bit skeptical about what you bought on the shopping trips you were on for the store. I wouldn't have bought half of the stuff you did. However, now that the Christmas sales are pretty much over, I will say that you both did a damn good job.

The store never looked better, thanks to my two daughters, and we made more money than I ever dreamed we would take in. And we're not done yet. The after holiday sales will make more money for the store. You both had good foresight in buying merchandise for the store. Thank you both again. I'm proud of you both, and now I know that the right decision was made when I put the store in your names. Dinner is on me tonight, order anything you want." We all laughed and Randy said,

"We were going to order what we wanted anyway dad." Again we all laughed including Big Ed.

New Year's Day arrived with everyone getting up at a different time. Three inches of snow greeted us. We all had breakfast at our own homes and then the kids got dressed to play in the snow with the dogs. The dogs loved the snow. They had more fun than the kids, who wrestled with the dogs. In between the horsing around, the four kids managed to build a snowman, his wife and two kids. They tied hard to make a dog but it didn't look like a dog no matter how hard they tried.

Later, when we were all together at my house, Patti had a table set for anyone who wanted to eat cold cuts, saurer kraut, kielbasa, warmed ham, chicken wings and many other finger foods. We usually had food like this set out and you could snack all day if you wanted. Randy, Big Ed, Syd and I took over the large TV in our den. The four kids took over the TV downstairs in the club room to play games and watch their favorite TV shows. Debbie and Patti were in the dining room, not too far from the food, going over their plans for Wilmington.

We gave them a list of restaurants and shops we had visited, plus some interesting places to visit for their upcoming weekend with all four children. Eddie and Linda were going there to practice and see what they could do to enhance their chances to maybe get into the U.S. Olympics. Coach Wilson thought that they have a pretty good chance to get noticed and maybe be able to get into the next Winter Olympics. It was worth a try. Linda and Eddie were trying very hard to make the grade and get noticed. I must admit that both Patti and I were set back by Eddie's interest in ice skating. He never showed any interest in anything but basketball. I took a good look at the two of them. Well, I hate to admit it, but they are growing up. They are young teenagers and no longer our little kids. They are both very attractive, not that childish look that they had yesterday... Yes, they are both young teenage adults now, and it looks like they ready to tackle the world. Patti and I have talked about this, and of course, Patti saw it coming before me. We're losing our kids. Linda was slender and a real beauty for her age. Eddie was a bit taller than Linda and he too was lean due to ice skating. They made an attractive couple on the ice. Coach Wilson said that he knew some people and would see to it that they got noticed. When the football games were over, the girls heated up some of the food, and we all sat down to snack and talk about the games, the snow family that the four kids built, and the trip coming up to Wilmington.

We bid Syd good night as he left to go home. And before Big Ed left, he kissed the children good night as they went to take their showers and go to bed. All the kids were spending the night at our house with both dogs. Big Ed wanted to talk to us without the children hearing. He had put $500 in each of their savings accounts and didn't want them to know about it just yet. Then he gave me and Randy an envelope and said that this was a bonus for doing such good work with store. Inside my envelope was a check for $1500; Randy got the same thing. We both protested that it was too much, but Big Ed wouldn't hear of our objections or complaints.

"We made damn good money during this holiday and this is the best way to say 'Thank You'. "I'd rather give it to you while I'm alive instead of the Government taking most of it when I die. Take it and enjoy yourselves." Patti and Debbie both got up and gave him a big kiss and thanked him again. Patti took our check and said to me,

"You know where this is going don't you hon? In the bank for their college education."

"Patti," said Big Ed, "spend that money on yourselves. Don't worry about the children's education. I have already provided for that with Syd. They are well cared for. So treat yourselves and don't worry about the children."

Patti and I were both speechless, as were Randy and Debbie. After Big Ed left, we began to talk and couldn't believe what we just heard. After the table was cleared off and everything put away, Randy and Debbie were going home. I kissed Debbie and shook hands with Randy, I held onto his hand, not wanting to let him go home. I really wanted to kiss him on the mouth, cheeks, and ears and put my tongue into his mouth, in his ear, tickle his tonsils suck his nipples and more; but I realized he had to go home with his wife, Debbie. I squeezed his hand not realizing how hard I griped his hand until I caught the surprised look on his face and eyes, and then I released my grip. I could tell by his eyes that he got my intent and message.

He gave me the familiar wink and they left. Before I went to bed, I was sitting by the fireplace finishing my drink and going over my life since I moved to Belvedere Road. I have a beautiful wife who loves me, two children who love me, a dog that loves me, and Randy. I know he loves me as I love him. I am a partner to a thriving hardware store, have an adoptive father who loves me, a good income, and college for my kids already taken care of. What more could I want? What more could I possibly want???? Randy with me more often. I wanted more of Randy. When I went to bed, Patti was waiting for me and of course that meant sex... I didn't disappoint her. We had a great night, but that night, I really wanted to be with Randy.

In the morning when I showered and got ready for work, I noticed that the snow was only on the grass. The streets were dry with little if any snow accumulation to amount to anything. When I entered the store, Big Ed and Randy had everything perking. The coffee was made and the store was comfortable heat wise. Big Ed was near the front of the store arranging some sale items as I poured myself a cup of coffee.

Randy was sitting on the edge of the desk and he grabbed my ass playfully saying, "Rough night last night?"

I almost whispered that it was when he left me. I wanted him to be with me. I also whispered that I wanted him so badly last night. But it couldn't be, I realized that.

Then Randy smiled and said that it won't be long, when the family goes to Wilmington, we will have the weekend together. Can you wait that long???

I hissed, "you bitch, can you wait that long?"

He answered, "Hell no! I want to be with you more than you will ever realize, but it just can't be. I miss you every minute when you're not here."

I knew he loved me, just as much as I loved him. I had a strong desire to reach over and give him a juicy kiss, but thought better of it. My hand was fingering his knee and I could see he was beginning to get aroused, so I gave him a hard squeeze and went in to help Big Ed.

Big Ed was almost finished when I got there to help and he said to me, "Do you two think you can handle the store without me today? I know you can but I have some things I want to take care of today and when the girls come in, I thought that I would leave. That Okay?"

I replied that it was fine, we weren't expecting too big of a crowd today and I was sure that the four of us could handle it. So he went in the back of the store, got his hat and coat, said a few words to Randy and left for the day. As it turned out, we were not busy at all. In fact we let the girls go home about 2 p.m., and they were happy to go. So we had the store to ourselves until we closed at 6 p.m. It was getting colder and we set the thermostat for the night, did our paperwork, made the bank deposit, straightened up the store a bit, and had a cocktail while we were kissing each other. Kisses led to other actions and we didn't care, we wanted each other and we did just that. We had each other and went home fully intoxicated with each other. I couldn't have been happier. I really love this guy and could never get enough of him. Oh happy day.

The next morning when we got to work, Randy and I shared a car. We weren't inside the door, when Andy came running in out of breath.

"Have you seen the morning paper," he gushed.

"No, we just got here. Why, what's wrong?" asked Randy.

"Mindi got arrested in Philadelphia over the weekend. Seems it's on a morals charge. One of her male model's parents called and told police that their son was accosted sexually by this woman."

"For Christ sake, can't the dumb kid keep his mouth shut? He probably only got a blowjob," said Randy. "He'll live."

Andy continued and said that the police got a very young looking cop to apply there for a modeling job and when Mindi pulled his zipper down, reach for his throbbing cock, that's when she was arrested. If he had pulled his zipper down and pulled his cock out, they couldn't touch her. But since she did it, they cuffed her. I said that I thought the whole thing smells.

Andy said "You're right. Her lawyer is claiming entrapment. And I think he's right. I thought that I'd let you know what's going on around here". We thanked him and Randy said if you learn anything else, let us know.

"Christ," said Andy, "I always suspected that she was a lipstick lesbian, but never told anyone. But this, it's almost too hard to believe."

"OK Andy" I asked, "What's a lipstick lesbian?"

"Sorry", said Andy, "I forgot about you two virgins. A Lipstick lesbian is a girl, who is shapely, dressed in the latest fashion, wears high heels, goes to the beauty shop and gets her hair styled. Extremely feminine, her make up is flawless. She wears good looking jewelry. In other words, they are very sexy to look at and talk to. You would never dream that they were lesbians. And they are tough as nails; you don't want to tangle with them. Like I said they are tough. We have a few come into the club on weekends and at first we thought they were in the wrong bar. Now we know them and they are nice girls. They added some class to the bar. Regular lesbians don't usually care about latest fashions and all that crap. They dress for comfort, mannish haircuts, jeans, plaid shirts and combat boots. That's way most of them dress very casual.

"Now, sweet thing, do you know the difference?"

"Yes I do, thank you." I answered, as I smiled at his delivery. Andy then left to get to work in the barber shop.

"Holy shit," said Randy, "seems like she was set up." We got busy in the store and time flew by. Randy and I couldn't discuss the Mindi case. We had more customers than we had expected, and that left little time to hash what little we knew. Andy popped his head in the store as he was leaving.

"Can't wait till I get downtown. The bars will be talking about nothing but Mindi." Andy was very excited about some additional news. Seems that when Mindi was arrested and put in jail, the police found out that Mindi's real name was Michael Martin and that Mindi was a young man posing as a woman all these years. Randy and I couldn't believe what we just heard. Andy said that it was all over the news, and we would probably get more details on the evening news.

The police have raided her shop on the mall, taking all her records and her lawyer is still claiming it to be a fowl. He said that the young lady has done nothing illegal and he is seeking an early court hearing. Andy popped into the store as he was leaving for the day and said that he couldn't wait to get downtown to Uncle Mary's. That place will be buzzing with gossip tonight.

"Those queens will crucify her or him, whatever. I'll keep you two posted with the latest dirt. Why don't you two come down to Uncle Mary's tonight? I promise you it will be a hoot." I begged off and so did Randy. Maybe another time we told him. "Okay, but you'll miss all the fun." And with that he was gone. Randy couldn't believe that Mindi was arrested and finding out that Mindi was Michael, well that was a double shock.

"Well", I said, "Michael sure as hell had me fooled and he made one hell of good looking gal. Remember when we first saw and met her. Andy said we were drooling over how beautiful she was and our only concern was to fuck her." Randy replied that Andy was right. We both talked about fucking her, and Andy said she was too high class for us.

"How little we know," I said. "What will happen now?" I questioned. Randy said that she will be held for trail on a morals charge of contributing to the delinquency of a minor; since the boy's parents complained to the police about her. He still feels that it was entrapment, and if her lawyer is any good, she could beat the rap. Forget the fact that the boy lied about his age. You know Mindi won't touch you as a client if you're underage. It will be interesting to see how this works out. What Mindi really needs is a sympathetic judge.

"Well, Andy will give us all the details that are not covered by the press," I said and added that I can't wait for tomorrow to come so Andy can brief us. "Will anything happen to her or him for impersonating a woman?" I inquired.

Randy said "he didn't think there was a law making it illegal to dress as a woman or vice versa. Randy added that he wasn't sure about his thoughts on this case. If it was illegal to dress and pose as a woman, or vice versa, all the gay bars would be raided and there would be one hell of a lockup. He said the he felt that she was OK on this point."

Randy and I closed the store early because business had slowed down. In fact, the entire strip was empty. It was cold and people weren't coming out to shop, so we didn't feel guilty about closing early; Big Ed also left early. Well, we shooed him home. We could handle the customers and I love being alone in the store with Randy. There's a feeling that prevails when we are there alone, that is missing when someone else is in the store. I can't explain it, but Randy has felt it too. Randy was tired and he sat at the desk to do the deposit. I cleared up the counters and as I looked in the office. There was Randy, sitting in a chair with his legs spread as far apart as they could go. This turns me on and he knew it. I told him about it some time ago. And the more I glanced his way, the hornier I got. Not being able to stand it anymore, I closed the office door, got on my knees directly in front of him and as I reached for his zipper and began to pull it down, he said,

"Are you going to rape me?" I grabbed his already hardened cock and said,

"You can't rape the willing. Is this what you're waiting for?" And I began to give him the best blowjob that I could. He moaned and squirmed until he slid off the chair onto the floor, tumbling on top of me where we became one. We remained there in each other's arms for quite some time. I could have easily spent the night here with Randy, kissing each other and whispering love messages in each other's ear. Moments like this are what mean so much to me. I don't get enough of these moments to suit me. And I know that Randy feels the same way, but we do the best we can without causing any suspicion. So far, so good. I really love this guy; I just don't get enough of him. As Dr. Lenhart said,

"You're doing the best you can with the hand you've been dealt."

The next day, we had the usual few people come, look around and buy some sale items at 9 a.m. By 10 a.m., the store was empty and Andy flew in like a whirlwind, very eager to tell what he learned last night. He went directly in the back, poured himself a coffee and came back to report everything.

"Those god damn queens. They act like they know everything, and the truth is they don't know anything."

"Who are you talking about?" I asked.

"Those fucking assholes at the bar. No matter when you go there, morning, noon or night, their asses are parked on the barstools. And they buy a drink in the morning and nurse it until later in the day or until some sucker buys them another. Someday, that bar will wise up and make them buy more drinks or leave. No more free ride all day long on two or three drinks. Yet to hear them talk, they are at all the places you hear about and read about. They all knew Mindi, some of them got blowjobs from her, and some of them had modeling jobs from her, and some knew that she would get in trouble for what she was doing. The truth is, none of them knew her, let alone get blowjobs or modeling jobs from her. She looked for handsome men, not that trash in the bars all day and night.

To hear them talk, you would think that she knew each of them and is a personal friend. The truth is these guys don't know her, never met her and wouldn't know her if they fell over her. They're bragging about her so that it will boast their popularity. Some screwballs will buy them a drink and ask questions about her. They make up stories because they have no real stories about her. I looked at Danny and he just shook his head in disbelief. Danny told Andy that this bull shit has been going on all day.

These dummies that are buying them drinks aren't smart enough to see their being fed a lot of bull shit." Then, Lulu came in followed by Danny, and was so shocked at the news. She always thought Mindi was an upscale lady, never dreaming that she was a he. The poor dear, wailed Lulu, what he must be going through at this time.

"Does he have any friends?" Andy answered that he thought he was always a loner. Lulu cried and then said,

"I'm going to see what he needs and buy them for him while he's in jail. Danny, will you take me there?"

"Sure Lulu, I'll be glad to." Andy then said that this is when I suspected that Danny and Lulu were an item. So I asked them and Lulu said that Danny was moving in with her and they were going apartment hunting for a larger place. When I left the bar for home, I noticed that the assholes were still on the same barstools that they were on all day; they were still giving false information and accepting drinks as though they were celebrities. I felt sick to my stomach and had to leave that phony crowd. I had a hard time falling asleep last night because those jerks had me upset."

"Don't let them get you upset," said Randy. "People like that usually hang themselves. People get wise to them and what they are and drop them like a hot potato. You're far above them; I wouldn't waste my time on them."

"Thanks Randy, I guess I needed that," said Andy.

As the 12th day of Christmas rolled around, Andy had the crew get ready to take down the Christmas decorations down. Everyone commented on how good it was to have a group who took the time and care to make a strip mall look so good. The articles that were rented went back with Frenchy to the Tri-county Decorating Company and all the rest of the decorations were packed up and stored in the drug store's basement. They have a lot of open space so they volunteered to keep it there until next year. Our wives came into the store and removed all traces of Christmas, they washed the windows and put some spring flowers around the windows along with big red hearts, gold and white cupids that Frenchy had bargained for, with his boss.

He got the Valentine Day supplies really cheap, along with red, white and gold-colored ribbons, which will brighten up the store a bit. In their spare time, Patti and Debbie were excited about the upcoming trip to Wilmington, Delaware. Patti would drive and they had a plan mapped out as to where they would eat, shop and sightsee. It was obvious that they were both excited about the upcoming trip. I was excited about their upcoming trip too.

Mindi was top news for about a day or two; then it became back page news. Too many international items took over the front pages. In fact, if you hadn't searched the paper from front page to last page, you would never had seen the article whereby the judge, in reviewing the evidence, threw the case out of court because of lack of evidence. The judge refused to let the prosecution admit her private files in court. The judge further ruled that living as a woman was not a crime, and that as far as he could see, there was no crime here. The young man in question admitted that he lied about his age to get to be a model. Mindi Martin aka Michael

Martin did nothing wrong and the judge agreed with her lawyer that this was entrapment; that the alleged assault took place in her apartment, private property and the cop, being of legal age, knew what would happen since this was set up by the police, so the judge threw the case out of court. We were glad to see the case dismissed. Andy, later on, found that Mindi was closing her Hamilton Mall office and moving it to the west coast where she had a small office. Once enlarged, it would be her main office.

Andy wanted to have a farewell party for Mindi. He figured it would take her about a month to get everything organized to leave for the west coast. Andy decided that he would have the party in his condo. He wanted Randy and me to attend. We agreed that we would be there. Our wives didn't know her so they weren't interested in going with us. I felt sorry for her that she had to close her business here and move to the West Coast, but I was happy for her; that she had a sympathetic judge who dismissed the case, and that she came out smelling like a rose. Lulu went shopping for some sundries that he might need; and poor Lulu, when she got to the jail, Mindi had been released and they had no forwarding address for her. Lulu left the shopping bag with Mindi's lawyer and told him to relay her good wishes to him. He also asked the lawyer to wish Mindi the best of luck when she moves out West if she doesn't get to see her before she leaves.

In the weeks that followed Christmas, our store took on a new complexion. Our wives finished painting and decorating for Valentine's Day and made the store inviting, not depressing, as they claimed it was before they made it over. I had to admit that brighter colors on the walls made a big difference. Big Ed said he liked the different look, and more power to the ladies. There were vases of artificial flowers scattered around and it added some color to a normally drab store. Then their forth coming trip to Wilmington was rapidly approaching. There were meetings with the coach, wardrobe people who had to make certain that there was plenty of freedom when they were skating, without losing the beauty of the costume in this remodeling. Patti loved doing this, but it was difficult to read how Debbie felt. There was something in her attitude that Patti couldn't put her finger on. It was her daughter that most of this decision making was about. She showed some interest, but it appeared that she showed very little enthusiasm. Debbie had applied for horse riding lessons that conflicted with the trip to Wilmington. So the riding lessons would have to wait until they got back from Delaware. Patti told me that she felt that this was the reason for her strange attitude. Debbie was so hyped on the horse riding lessons.

The Wilmington trip was very successful, according to Coach Wilson. Some of the Olympic Representatives were there, and their comments about Linda and Eddie were encouraging. With some hard work and more training, they would be considered for the Winter Olympics in two years. Both Patti and Debbie were ecstatic over the news. The Olympic Committee wanted to know who they could contact as donors for the kids, to help defray the expenses. They were given all the stores on the mini strip. We didn't anticipate any problems along this line. All of the store owners or managers knew the kids through the hardware store. Debbie was happy because she could pursue her horse riding lessons at the Trent Riding Academy. The riding academy is owned and operated by Jake and Gloria Trent, who also own and operate Trent Valley Farms, which is about seventy acres on your way to I-95. And Patti was happy because she could devote more time to the kids skating needs such as make-up, hair and costumes.

This would be right up her alley. Randy and I had really enjoyed the girl's trip to Wilmington. We spent every night that we could together. We only had to care for the dogs for the weekend that they were gone, and that was no problem. Randy and I ate out every night with Big Ed, who enjoyed treating us and doing his very best to spoil us. We were already spoiled and he knew it. We were home early at night and opened the store at 9 am each day. It's hard to believe we had opened the store on time when you realize the rough night we had once we went to bed, and I loved every minute of it as did Randy. We both hated to see it end. I began thinking more and more of how it would be to have Randy with me all the time. I don't know if Randy ever thought of it, he never mentioned it. But I've had it on my mind more and more here of late. One day when we're in a cozy, talking mood, I'll bring up the subject matter again. We both feel the same way about our wives, and I know that neither of us would do anything to hurt our families. But there is this gnawing at my inners and I can't seem to get rid of it. Maybe he can help. If Randy can't help me maybe Dr. Lenhart could be of some help.

While in the store, I noticed a well-dressed man of about forty years old or so, looking at items in the store and more than once, I caught him watching me… so I approached him and asked if I could help him.

"No," he replied, "I'm just browsing around looking for something unusual for a gift. If I need help, I will call you." I remember seeing him in the store before and now that I think of it, I always caught him staring at me. So feeling bold, I approached him and said,

"I've seen you in the store several times and you always leave empty handed. Is there something I can do for you?" He put out his hand and said,

"My name is Al Betz, you've heard of the Betz Department Stores? My mother owns all three of them in this area. We have one in the Hamilton Mall. You've heard the slogan "Best Buys are at Betz." I nodded that I've heard of them, and have shopped there.

"Nice stores, always find something to buy."

"Mother would love to hear that," replied Al.

"Saw you a good while ago at Uncle Mary's way before Christmas. You were going to the men's room and it looked like you were struggling to get through the crowd." I said that I don't remember seeing him, since there was a big crowd. Al said "I felt your ass on your way to the men's room. Very nice and on your way back to your booth, I reached out and felt your dick." Now I remembered! That someone gave me the once over with his hands at the bar. "That too was very nice, I invited you to join me at the bar and have a good time. You answered that you were having a good time with your friends at the booth. I said if you change your mind, come back. You never did. I was so impressed by you, your good looks, and the way you handle yourself, that I asked Chuck to find out who you were, where you lived, worked and so forth."

"Who's Chuck and why the interest in me?"

"See the guy at the front of the store in a red sweater?" Al said. "That's Chuck. He's a private investigator. My mother has hired him to keep an eye on me and let her know where I go, who I see, and what I do and how I spend my time when I'm out. She wants me to get married and have children. What a shock she would get if she knew her son was out sucking cock whenever he could. I pay Chuck so much money each month so that my mother will never know the truth about me." My face must have registered my concern and questions on my mind.

"Chuck is gay and he knows I am. I'm engaged to be married next summer. I'm bisexual and I do want a wife and children - ON MY TERMS, not my mother's. Chuck feeds my mother what she wants to hear. If mother had her way, I would have been married months ago. Chuck and I have had sex together, and at times a three some." I had a quizzical look on my face when Al said,

"What does this mean to you? Well, I'd like to get to know you better, maybe have dinner, and come my condo for drinks and who knows what will happen next. You're the kind of guy I'd like my mother to meet so she would know that I'm not hanging out with some riff raff."

"That's all nice and flattering but I'm a married man, happily married with two children".

"I know all that," Al said," I know that you and your partner live next door to each other, Randy also has two children. I also know that you and Randy are co-owners of this store. He's another one that I would like give a blowjob to."

"Al," I said, "I'm not gay, neither is Randy. We were at Uncle Mary's because we hired some men who hang out there, to decorate this mall for Christmas. They did a great job and we became friendly with them. They invited us to the Christmas show and we went and took out wives. We had a nice time and enjoyed ourselves."

"I know all that," said Al, "But it doesn't hurt to put all your cards on the table. Most men like a good blowjob and that's what I'm offering you."

"Well, I'm sorry. I'm not interested. I can't speak for Randy, but I'm almost positive he would say no."

"Well, no harm in trying and no hard feelings, OK?"

"No hard feelings. I've got to help some of our customers, so if you'll excuse me." I then went to the rear of the store as Al and Chuck left and I began to wait on some customers. When we had a breather, Randy came up alongside of me and said,

"What was that all about?" So, we had some time and I told him, in detail, my conversation with Al Betz while his private detective looked on.

Randy laughed and said, "Why didn't you kick his ass and throw him out?" Randy laughing said.

"You know that I am not aggressive," I quietly added.

"You should do to him what you do to me. Not aggressive? Ha!" whispered Randy, so that no one would hear but me.

"If I did that to him," I whispered, "he would never go home. I thought I did the right thing. I sure don't want to meet his mother." Randy gave me an inviting pat on the ass and said,

"If he comes back, call me," and he went into the office with Big Ed.

Days went into weeks and weeks went into months. Linda and Eddie were spending most of their free time skating with Coach Wilson, who had glowing reports about how well they were doing. It was almost a sure thing that they would get the nod for the Winter Olympics in Canada in two years' time. Patti was on cloud nine since Debbie might not want to get involved thus leaving Patti in complete charge.

Debbie on the other hand was so wrapped up in her horseback riding that she had little time for anything else. Her lessons were Monday, Wednesday and Friday, but she was at the academy almost every day. Of course, she had to buy an outfit suitable for horseback riding and she did look very well in it. Debbie was an extremely beautiful woman. When in a crowd, she was a head turner. Her perfect size nine, along with her auburn hair and baby blue eyes, made her stand out wherever she went.

Her clothes were expensive and she wore them well. So when she bought some horse riding clothes, they were most expensive but money was the least of her concerns. On the other hand, Patti had noticed a slight but increasing change in Debbie's personality. She began finding fault with Randy, little, picky things at first, then little by little, she became more aggressive with her complaints about Randy. Nothing really serious, just complaints. Patti would speak to me about this because she could find no fault with Randy. Patti felt that he was the perfect husband, handsome, good looking, well educated, the perfect father, in fact Patti could find no fault with Randy no matter how hard she looked. Then she thought, I guess you really have to live with a person to realize what their faults are. She dismissed that thought thinking, I still think he's a perfect person. And Debbie has no real complaint about Randy.

Big Ed called his two sons together one morning when the business was slow, and the two gals could handle the shop. He had been getting mail from many of the wholesalers announcing the coming spring shows in March.

He wanted his two sons to handle the buying at the shows since their performance for Christmas was outstanding. He still couldn't believe that they did so well with their purchases. Both shows were in March; one in Richmond, VA., and the other was in Brooklyn, N.Y. They were two weeks apart. The dealers planned it that way. I let Randy make all the reservations. We would drive to Richmond, but fly to New York. Each show was three days plus travel time. Randy decided that the first day would be travel time, and then we should wrap up the show in two days since a lot of the items are not suitable for our hardware store. Then we could head home a day early. This should hold true for both shows and sounds good to me. I trust Randy with my life.

When I got home from work this night, Patti showed me an article in the paper. A picture of the Trent Riding Academy students; including eight women and one man and their names. There was a picture of Jake and Gloria Trent, owners of the Trent Valley Farms where the riding academy was located. Jake Trent was a handsome six foot tall man, who could have played football in his day. He looked about forty to forty five, although Debbie said he was about fifty or fifty one years old. His wife was a beautiful, petite brunette and you couldn't tell her age.

"Jake Trent is a hunk, isn't he?' I said to Patti.

"Yes he is, his wife is also a looker," she replied.

"Well, I hope this is what she wants. She seems preoccupied here lately and I can't put my finger on what's bugging her."

"I haven't noticed anything different with her," I said. Then Patti replied,

"You're never here to see her mood swings and how little things upset her."

"Really!!!, Debbie???" I said in disbelief.

"Yeah, I've noticed some minor irritations going back for several months. It's getting a bit more serious here of late, especially with Randy. She's been finding all kinds of fault with him. Every now and then she'll open up and feed me a complaint or two then clams up. I listen but I definitely do not agree with her. Randy is a perfect husband in my eyes." I silently agreed with her one hundred percent. Randy is perfect in my eyes too.

"Too bad," I commented. "Any idea what this is all about?" I asked?

"Well, yes. I wasn't going to say anything, but tonight when the kids are in bed, you and I can have a discussion about what I think might be bugging her." With my curiosity slightly aroused, I couldn't wait for this evening to learn more about this problem. Later that evening, when the kids were in bed, Patti made us a drink and we sat cozily in the den, with the TV playing, where we could talk. Patti started by saying,

"Debbie thinks there is something going on between you and Randy." This hit me like a ton of bricks.

"What!" I half whispered, the adrenaline shot up my spine and I had the hairs on the back of my neck stand up, and I think my heart stood still. Trying to keep my composure I said,

"Has she lost her mind? What would make her say such a thing?" Patti laughed and said,

"Del, it's so far-fetched. Debbie feels that since you two have become friendly, Randy is too nice to her, he gives her everything she wants and because of that, she feels that there is something between you two." Patti laughed again.

"For Christ sake," I said. "What's he supposed to do, make her go to work and earn her own money? Maybe she'd be happier if he beat her now and then. What the hell's she thinking of? I could understand if he never gave her anything, but he bends over backwards to keep her happy. What more can he do?" Patti agreed with everything I said.

"I told her she was crazy for her attitude." Patti continued, "I pointed out his good values as a husband, a father, a provider for her, the children and a good business man." I said, "Look at your home, it's a fashion plate. You want for nothing. Do you know how many women would give their eye teeth to have what you have? You have your own car, your own bank account; you come and go as you please. He works all day. What more do you want from him?" Debbie answered me by saying,

"There's something there. I can't put my finger on it, but I feel there's a reason for him being so nice to me. Something's wrong." Then Patti was very serious when she said,

"Del, I don't believe there is anything going on between you and Randy. I met you when I was in my second year at college and fell in love with you. I made up my mind then that you were the man for me. And I was right. I married you and have never had any regrets. And I never had and still don't regret my marriage to you. You have been a faithful husband, father and provider for me and the children, and I'll love you till the day I die. I don't agree with Debbie. I can't see anything going on between you and Randy; but if there is, I'm not aware of it nor am I going to look for anything. I know that you're very close to each other, but you're in business together and you're both making money.

If there is something going on between you two, as I said, I'm not aware of it and I'm not going to bird dog you to find out. Now if it was another woman involved, I wouldn't sleep until I found out who she was and then I'd settle with her properly. I love Randy... we all do. The children idolize him and they are happier here than anywhere we have lived. I too have a beautiful home, money in the bank, my own car. What more could a woman want? I'm very happy with the life we have together and I don't want anything to ruin it. I'm beginning to think she has a problem and it's her problem, not ours. I have backed you when you wanted to leave Pennsylvania and move here. And guess what? No regrets on my part. I love where we live, the area, the kids are happy here. We have a home that is beautiful and most important, I still love you as I did in college, only more so.

My sex life with you is fine; I could never complain that I've been neglected."

I kissed my understanding wife as I often do and asked her to keep this conversation between the two of us, and she agreed. I, of course, wanted to have a conversation with Randy but how would I do it? I wouldn't want him to blow up at Debbie and have a free-for-all. Then there would be hell to pay and possibly the breakup of two supposedly happy families. I want to think about how to handle this and decide if I want to tell him or maybe just let it ride. I don't want Randy to get hurt. I love him too much for that. I'll have to decide what to do, if anything. If worse comes to worse, I'll call Dr. Lenhart and get some professional advice. He did caution us when we spoke with him that this utopian life might come to a rapid ending.

God, I hope not, I love Randy so much that I hate to think of life without him. There would be no life without him. Well, time will tell. How would I tell him? He might get mad enough to do something stupid. No, Randy is not a stupid person, yet, you don't know what he would do when he is really angry. Come to think of it, I have never seen him angry, or ever lose his temper. Dear God, what gave her such an idea? Did we do something careless or what? I wracked my brain trying to see if we did something or said something that would trigger her statements. I couldn't find anything that we would have done to cause this. I want to tell Randy and yet, I'm afraid of what he might do. Our trust in each other is beyond reproach, as is our feelings and love for each other.

Randy and I would both do everything in our power to keep our relationship between the two of us a deep guarded secret. Yet here is a threat that we will probably have to deal with. I don't know when, or how, but I can see it coming to a head, and I know that I'm not ready for it. Randy, I'm really afraid to tell him, but he must be told. Debbie can't confront him with this cold turkey. He must be warned and ready for whatever she tells him. I can't let him get hit out of the blue with accusations. I can't think straight; my mind is a blur. Maybe after a good night's sleep, I can approach him and discuss what has happened tonight. I've got to tell him, and soon.

Sleep did not come easy tonight. I relived my conversation with Patti over and over again. And when I finally did dose off, my sleep was not peaceful. I tossed and turned, my sleep was fitful; all kind of crazy things were running through my mind. I was glad to wake up and take my shower and get ready for the task that was waiting for that morning at work. Again, I cautioned Patti to keep mum about our conversation and please, don't antagonize Debbie. Forget she told you anything. I told her that I loved her, kissed her goodbye and left for the shop. As I drove to the store, my love for Randy was getting stronger and stronger. I knew that when I see him, I'd want to hold him in my arms so tightly that I could hear him complain that my grip was too tight.

I wanted to smother him with kisses and just be with him in my arms. I really love this guy, and more so now than ever before. I couldn't think of him being hurt by his wife and her suspicions. Any pain he has, I have. I want to protect him, shield him from her. Oh why does she have to be so damned clever and suspect that something is going on? I can see that this is going to be a long day for Randy and me. I can't let him hurt her in any way and by the same token, I can't let her hurt him. I've got to protect him as best as I can. I love him, and I will protect him to the best of my ability. As I parked the car, the brief walk to the store seemed like I would never get there. The walk seemed longer and longer, although it was the same short walk I have traveled every day.

When I entered the store, the gals were busy working some stock, Big Ed was in the office and Randy was down the basement, everyone was cheerful but me. I tried not to let them know that I had the weight of the world on my shoulders. It was so hard, almost painful to look at Randy and not throw my arms around his neck and profess my love for him.

The question of Petey came up. No one has seen nor heard from him since before Christmas when he worked about six hours, wanted paid in cash and left. We didn't know how to get in touch with him. So Randy and I decided that if and when he showed up for work, we would tell him that we had enough help and didn't need his services any longer. I think he got that message when he found our wives and children were helping out at the store. We never heard from or saw him again - just as well. I got Randy aside and told him that I have something very important and private to speak to him about.

"Could we get away from the store for a while some time during the day?"

"Sure, we could take a long lunch, dad won't mind." Clear it with Big Ed before we leave. Randy agreed and I couldn't wait for our lunch break to arrive. I was on pins and needles. We drove out to Edgewater Dam to the restaurant and ordered lunch to go. Randy and I drove to a very scenic spot, and ate lunch in the car, overlooking the dam. I wasn't hungry so I nibbled at my lunch.

"So what's the big secret you have to talk about that you couldn't tell me in the store?" I reached for his hand, squeezed it and quickly withdrew so that no one would see what I had done.

"Randy, you know that I love you more than I can ever say. I would die for you and this conversation is the hardest thing I have ever had to do in my life."

Randy got white and his lips began to quiver and he whispered,

"Del, are you leaving me? Is our love over?"

"Hell no Randy, I will never leave you." The color slowly crept back into his face and he said,

"Christ, that's the worst thing that could happen to me. Without you, I have no purpose."

"No, my love for you is stronger now than it's ever been," I replied, and said a silent prayer for guidance so that I would say the right things. I told him, as gently as I could, about the conversation between Patti and me concerning Debbie. He didn't say anything after I finished talking. Just sat there looking at his coffee cup.

"You know that my love for you is the most important thing in my life, Del. Without you, there would be no reason for me to keep living. You know how we both feel about our wives and children, but I don't think I could live without you."

"Don't say that Randy. I feel the same way you do, but there's a higher authority than you or me, that will decide when we leave this earth."

"Debbie has done this before," sighed Randy. "When I worked in the insurance office, I had several employees under my supervision. She did accuse me of running with one of the girls, who I was training for a managerial position, as I was instructed to do by the home office. Her name was Rose Titus, and she was sharp. The home office knew that three key people were planning to leave and asked me to train her - which I did. She sat near my desk and would answer my phone when it rang and I wasn't near my desk. I planned it this way so that she would get and answer my calls and learn how to handle them. This is part of the on-the-job training the company offers.

Debbie called several times, Rose answered the phone and that put a bug in Debbie's head that we were a twosome, Rose and me. Debbie didn't come right out and accuse me; she would drop little hints that could be taken two ways. And when I finally caught on to what she was saying, I'd approach the issue and she would back off saying, I misunderstood her. This went on until Rose got promoted and was transferred to the Harrisburg, PA., office. Then I got transferred down here the following year and I never heard from Rose again. Now Debbie is starting this crap all over again, but this time with you." I picked up my lunch and tossed it into a trash can nearby, and got back into the car. I had a hard time checking my tears. I didn't want Randy to see me cry but he did and he pulled me close to him in the car and said,

"We have done nothing to alert her or cause her to be suspicious of us. She has some sort of problem that is doing this to her. Please don't cry, you've done nothing, neither have I." And he held me close with his arms around me. A lot of the people who were having lunch at the dam, left to return to work. Very few people were there to see us, and I didn't care. I couldn't stand to see Randy hurt this way. And I detected a tear or two in his eyes, and I really wanted to take him in my arms and make passionate love to him. We both knew where we stood with each other, and even though I couldn't make love to him there, I let my hands and fingers do talking and he understood what I meant. I really love this man more now than ever before. We went back to work and agreed not to discuss this at work.

Randy felt that I should tell Patti about our talk concerning Rose, and to play it aloof should Debbie begin talking about us again. Don't let on she knows anything about Rose - play it cool. While back at work, we were doing things in a mechanical manner. Our thoughts were on Debbie and her statements. My thoughts were on Randy and how much I really loved him, and how difficult it was to work with him so close to me and I couldn't touch him. It was sheer torture. Andy stopped by before he went home and reminded us that he was having a farewell party for Micki tonight at 7 p.m. She would be there at 7:30 p.m. I forgot all about it, as did Randy.

"Can we bring anything?" I asked.

"No, everything is under control. Just be there." And he was off. So when we finished work at the store and got set up for the next day with the cash drawers and the bank deposit, we both rushed home, showered, and since the wives didn't care to go, we left.

We arrived a bit after 7:00 pm, and Andy met us at the door, shoved a scotch and water in our hands and began introducing us to some of the people we didn't know. Andy had about thirty five or forty people there and it was beginning to look like a really festive party. At about 7:45 p.m. the doorbell rang, and when Andy opened it, there was a delivery man with two dozen long stem roses in a box for Andy. Andy tipped the guy and opened the box, took out a note, and read it aloud,

> "Dearest Andy and friends; how sweet and thoughtful of you to give me a farewell party before I leave for L.A. The last few weeks here in Maryland have been humiliating for me. Even though I won the case, the stain is and always will be present. When you get this note and roses of love, I will be high in the sky heading for the West Coast. Thank you and all of my friends who are with you. I love you and will always love you. If by chance any of you come to L.A., please look me up. My address has not changed. All my love, Micki."

Amid murmurs of regrets, and sighs of disappointment, everyone seemed to understand her decision. Andy managed to get a vase of water and arrange the roses on his piano. Shortly after the note reading, someone sat at the piano and began playing Broadway show tunes. Well after that, the piano was the place to be and hear everyone singing. It turned out to be a delightful evening and one we hated to leave but, we had to work the next day. Randy, Big Ed and I agreed to work on Sundays for a few weeks to unload some of the holiday items, so we left around 11:00 p.m.

On the drive home, Randy said that he hardly slept the night before because of Debbie. I could tell that he was worried about her and what damage she could create for us and for both families. I tried to comfort him by asking how he handled it before with Rose. He replied that with Rose, she stopped needling him when Rose was transferred, as I predicted. She must have realized that I told her the truth and then I got transferred too, she had no argument. Then I looked at him and saw tears coming down his face and that just broke my heart. I had to hold him and caress him.

"I love you, no matter what. Always remember that. I love you." He put his arm around me and kissed my cheek while he was driving. He pulled off the road as soon as he could and really gave me a kiss to remember. We sat there for about fifteen minutes, maybe longer, and we both shed a few tears. We both agreed that she would not come between us and that we would not admit to anything. What did she know? Nothing. Because Randy gave in to her every whim, this was wrong?

We left the parking area both feeling a lot better, knowing that we had done nothing wrong. She was suspicious because her husband treated her too well? She was guessing. If it ever came up in conversation, we would both call it her imagination. We were ready for her. Then Randy remembered that the last time she had this problem, he made an appointment for her with the family physician, Dr. Louis Stiller. She never kept the appointment. Randy said,

"I think I'll call Dr. Stiller and see if he can get her in for a routine check-up." I could see that Randy was gearing up for a showdown with her and then he began to cry again saying that he loved her so much and didn't want to hurt her in anyway. I had my hands full with him this time, and it was a difficult thing to do because I know how much he loves her. I felt the same way about my wife. I would never do anything to hurt her or my kids. It seemed like a showdown was heading in our direction, for all of us. God, I hope   that   I   am   wrong   about   this.

CHAPTER 19 - Richmond, VA

So much was happening: getting ready for the first spring show; Randy's appointment with Dr. Stiller concerning Debbie; Debbie's riding lessons; and Patti getting ready for the next ice show with Linda and Eddie. All of this left more time for Randy and me to be together. I couldn't wait to get on the road with him, to get him away for all this worry, to comfort him at night, just the two of us. I needed him, he needed me, and we needed each other. Randy and I talked about our children on our way to Virginia. Linda would be fifteen next year, Josh would be seventeen, Eddie would be sixteen and Bobby would be fifteen. My gosh, we have been neighbors for almost eight years.

"Christ how time flies," Randy said. "Do you realize that if you wouldn't have taken that promotion with Lamont Reality, we would have never met and God knows where we both would be today? We wouldn't know each other." I said that if I had turned down the promotion, I'd be stuck in some burg, not knowing anyone and be bored to shit. Randy laughed. It was good to hear him laugh again.

"Once around the block, you'd have found a friend to play with, like me." I playfully poked him on his arm and said.

"No baby, there is no one else like you. You're one of a kind and I thank God every day that I got you first. Of course, I would have a hell of a good time trying to find someone like you." And I had to laugh; I couldn't control my humor any longer. Then he jabbed me in the ribs and we both laughed. It was really good to have him laugh again. In a serious moment, Randy said that he paid Dr. Stiller a visit and explained what was going on with Debbie. Dr. Stiller said that he looked up her file and saw that she had an appointment several years ago and cancelled it. I called her to reschedule, but she felt fine and wasn't interested. I think it's time I give her another call. This time, I won't take no for an answer. She's way past due for a check-up. He promised to keep my visit a secret.

My objective on this trip was to have fun with Randy, make him laugh and forget all the troubles that have been bothering him or us for the past few weeks. The trip to Richmond was a little over four hours driving time. We didn't care. It could have been eight or ten hours, we didn't care. Randy and I were together, we could talk about our problems, stop and get a bite to eat, take our time and get there when we get there. Randy had made reservations at the Richmond Arms, just across the street from the spring craft show.

Once we signed into the hotel, we went ahead and registered with the craft show. They were open for registrations the day before the show began, which is customary according to Randy. Once you have been to a show, the rest is always the same. You get a credit card with your name and account number on it. This is your pass go enter the show and buy what you want in your firm's name. Same routine we used before. Even though we were in a different city for a new craft show, Debbie was the topic of our conversations. There were, we thought, some serious issues to be handled. Then on the other hand, we could simply treat this as a figment of her imagination and dismiss it as nothing. This is what we plan to do, since she has no proof, just suspicions.

Randy and I didn't feel like taking in the sights of Richmond, we were happy to retire to our room where we could be alone with each other. Once in our room, Randy grabbed me in a loving embrace, then as we were kissing, he loosened my belt, slid both hands down inside my briefs and gently, but firmly caressed each cheek of my ass and slowly pulled my cheeks towards him.

"Welcome to Richmond, Del." What a beautiful welcome!!! After we had sex, we went to dinner and decided to call it a night. We did just that, retired to our room for the night. I thought that the Debbie issue would hang over Randy and prevent him from having good sex with me. Nothing was further from the truth. We enjoyed the best sex we have ever had, and we were both exhausted. What a pleasure it was to lay back in his arms with my arms around his waist totally relaxed. This was heaven. Randy wasn't too concerned about Debbie at this time, and I was damn glad. He didn't deserve this and if I helped him forget her in any way, I was glad of it. I had him in my arms, I was holding him a bit tight, he was mine, and I had him and didn't want to let him go.

Selfish, I know, but that's the way I felt. What was it that I learned in law class, 'Possession is nine tenths of the law'. Well, I had him and unfortunately I couldn't apply the law here. Nice thought though. We fell asleep in each other's arms and I never felt happier. When the alarm went off in the morning, I really didn't want to get up, I would have been happy to spend the day in bed with Randy, but there was work to be done. After we showered together, and while I was washing his back and privates, we played drop the soap. When Randy and I were finished playing, we got dressed and went to get some breakfast, and then entered the spring show. We did find some unusual items for the hardware store, lamps, modern and period. We found some very modern fixtures for bathrooms and kitchens as well as accompanying clocks and kitchen accessories.

We both felt that these would be a big hit with our wives as well as the women shoppers in the neighborhood. Randy and I turned the bend on the second floor and ran into about an acre of the most beautiful silk flowers I have ever seen. Randy was surprised too at the sheer beauty of all these silk flowers. We bought more than we really intended to buy, but they were so appealing. We went hog wild with our buying spree. We bought huge plastic tubs to display all the flowers in. They were selling enameled pots and pans in various colors to brighten up a drab kitchen. We bought some of them too.

Randy and I left the showrooms early and headed for a nearby bar to get a drink or two. After enjoying our drinks, we decided to get a bite to eat and call it a day. Nothing made me happier than to call it a day, when I could have Randy to myself. He didn't say anything but I could tell that he felt the same way about me. We took showers to get some of the craft dust and dirt off of us, and then we got into bed nude under a thin sheet and watched some TV. Soon, the TV became boring and we became interested in each other. We began making love to each other. I kissed his eyes, nose, lips, neck, ears, and nipples and licked other parts of his body with my tongue.

He responded as I knew he would. We began to explore each other and he got hard first, then I followed suit. He began licking my nipples, then down to my navel and finally to my rock hard cock. By this time, we were in sixty nine position. Randy had me so hot that I couldn't control my urge to cum, as much as I wanted us to cum together. I shot first followed by Randy, a second or two later. We laid here, holding each other and basking in the after-glow of our hot sex. Randy and I never have made love like this before, but I knew it would happen again. It was so wonderful. I couldn't wait for us to do it again.

When we climaxed, we were one and I didn't want it to end. We had a scotch and water, watched the late news and fell asleep embracing one another. I really love this guy so much. Thank God I took the promotion and moved to Maryland when I did, otherwise I would never have met Randy; and my life would have been so boring. I can't picture my life without Randy.

The second day was cloudy, threatening rain which never came. We did some shopping on three more floors and bought some electrical tools for men, some craft sets for wood working buffs, some hobby sets for glass workers who like to make lamps, glass frames, and other forms of art work involving colored glass. We also bought some other supplies that we needed for the store, and quit early as we did the day before.

After a few drinks, we had something to eat and headed for the hotel. We had a repeat of last night. What a wonderful way to end a perfect day, in each other's arms, soothing the fears that we felt might happen. We felt something might happen but it never did come. Randy does sleep warm and very comfortable in my arms. He falls asleep first and we are embraced in each other arms as I lay there watching him sleep, so innocent, so beautiful and so inviting. How could anyone want to harm him? When I awoke in the morning before the alarm went off, I shut off the alarm, slide out of bed and went to the bathroom.

I returned to bed and saw Randy sleeping peacefully as he did last night. I quietly got back into bed and admired his sculptured body. Looks like he's sporting a semi-hard on. Well... I ever so gently moved my fingers down his chest, navel and finally down his cock shaft. It didn't take long for him to be fully erected. Then, I placed my hands under his soft, sweet ass; one hand per cheek. Then I kneed my way between his legs and they separated easily. Once in position, I began to give him a gentle blowjob. As his cock got harder, my thrusts became more rapid. He lazily opened his eyes and appraised the scene. I could tell that he was about to explode, and he did, but I didn't stop. I kept on rubbing my tongue around his cock head. I don't know how long a guy can bear this painful pleasure; but I wanted to see how long Randy could endure the sensation. He couldn't stand it anymore and I was deaf to his pleas to stop. So he finally pulled my mouth off his cock. He sighed as he lay back on the bed. Then he scooted down to where I was and when our faces were close to each other, he reached his hand around the back of my neck, pulled me closer to him and gave me the best French kiss I ever had. De Ja Vu.

"What are you trying to do, kill me?" asked Randy.

"No", I replied, "What makes you say that?"

"How much of that painful pleasure do you think I can take?"

"I don't know, I'm trying to find out, but you're not a good subject," I replied.

Randy said, "Look at my cock... it's swollen, especially around the head."

"It's that much more for me to play with and have fun with." I took his cock in my hand and apologized for causing it to be swollen. Then I kissed it. Randy gave me a playful smack across the rump and said we'd better get ready for business today. I was getting ready for the craft show today, but my mind was on what a wonderful weekend we have had in bed. This was our third and last day in Richmond. I felt pretty good that I managed to take Randy's mind off his wife for three days, but all good things must come to an end. He would have his hands full when he got home, or maybe not. She hasn't said a word to Randy, or accused him of anything. Maybe the trip home, when we get there, will be uneventful. Let's hope for the best. Neither of us was in any hurry to get home. We had such a wonderful time in Richmond. Randy and I were discussing the next craft show in Brooklyn, N.Y. Randy had decided to take the train to Brooklyn. We would be there in about two and one half hours. I liked this better than flying. There was always so much confusion when you fly. Randy was sorry that he didn't mention this to me before. I put his mind at ease; I said,

"Randy, if you wanted to walk I'd walk with you just so long as we were together."

"I knew I had a gem when I snagged you," replied Randy.

"We are not walking, but riding in a clean train."

When we arrived at our homes, the children were all doing their homework, Patti was making some chocolate chip cookies and Debbie was out. The children were at my house because of the chocolate chip cookies. We sat down in the kitchen with Patti and briefed her on our conversations about Debbie. Our conversation was low because the children were in the den doing homework and we didn't want them to hear us. Patti served us a good hot cup of coffee that both of us wanted and along with the cookies, it was perfect. Patti agreed to keep what we told her to herself; even if Debbie claimed to know something, not to believe her, she was only fishing for some information. She knew nothing... there was nothing to know. Patti felt so sorry for Debbie. She's torturing herself with suspicions, like she did with Rose. If only I could reach her and talk to her.

"NO, please don't even try," Randy cried, "You could do more harm than good. It will have to work itself out as it did with Rose." Patti agreed. You could see the pain Patti was going through. Debbie and Patti have been closer than two sisters and it has got to be hard to sit by and watch this take place...you feel so helpless... And poor Randy...what must that poor man be going through?

"Del, stand by him. He really needs a true friend now."

"Patti, he has you, and me. You know I'll be with him, more than anyone."

Monday morning when Randy had a few minutes, he called Dr. Stiller and the doctor didn't want to talk over the phone. He suggested that Randy come see him that afternoon between 2 and 3 p.m. Randy agreed, and when he got back to the store around 4:30 p.m., we would go out for a bite to eat around 5:00 p.m. The girls and Big Ed could handle the store. They were not that busy. While Randy and I were toying with our food, Randy began telling me what Dr. Stiller had to say. He definitely suspects some manic-depressive illness commonly called bipolar disorder. She goes through periods of depression, followed by periods of excitement or happy times. This type of illness is usually hereditary. Then, Dr. Stiller asked if Randy knew of her family, and if anyone in her family had a similar type illness. Randy didn't know.

"When she is in these periods of depression, she could be extremely dangerous to herself and loved ones or anyone around her at the time. When she is in a bipolar state, we advise the family members to remove all medications from her sight. Remove temptation. Try to remove all sharp objects such as scissors, knives or forks, any sharp objects. These measures are extreme, but until we know the degree of the illness, we must be cautious. I don't think Debbie is that sort of a threat yet, but she could snap in a heartbeat. Some patients are suicidal. Again, I don't think Debbie is, but we must be sure. I want to see her again and check her more thoroughly. I have set an appointment for her in three weeks."

Randy looked at his pocket calendar and said, "That's the week we'll be in N.Y. for a craft show."

Dr. Stiller then said, "Good, I want to see her alone."

Back at the store, we had closed for the night and I was leaning over the office desk, looking at a map of Brooklyn when I felt some hot breath on my neck. Randy was also reading the map over my shoulder.

I kiddingly said, "If you continue to get closer to me, and breathe your sexy hot breath down my back, you'll have me hot and bothered with a hard on."

To which he replied, "If I have to have one, why can't you?" I slide my hand behind my back and felt that he did indeed have a raging hard on. That was all she wrote. After some glorious sex, we did some paper work for the next morning and lazily headed home.

CHAPTER 20 - Brooklyn, NY

The Brooklyn N.Y. trip was here before we knew it. Patti was almost full time with all four children and she loved every minute of it. Debbie was devoting as much time as she could to her riding lessons, so she was gone most of the time. Randy and I got the shock of our lives. This craft show was fabulous. Four entire floors were devoted to Easter - colorful baskets, ceramic bunnies, toys for children of all ages. Beautiful plush bunnies to the mechanical and musical bunnies, all shapes, sizes and colors. Something for everyone, no matter the age. We spent two days shopping in the Easter Maze. We also spent lots of money there. They also were selling pectin jelly beans, chocolate covered filled eggs, marshmallow duck eggs, as well as other Easter candies. Randy said he couldn't remember the store ever selling candy. And I quipped,

"Well, there's a first time for everything. We'll either make a bundle of money, or lose our shirts."

The best time for me at these craft shows was when we were alone in our hotel room and in each other's arms. To have Randy in my arms nude and horny was more than I could ask for. He still had his sex appeal to me. And after so much sucking and fucking, moaning and groaning, I still want him and he wants me. This was heaven on earth for me. I have cherished all those special memories and will take them with me to my grave. Our third day in Brooklyn was spent sightseeing. There is so much to do and see in N.Y., and we tried to do most of it in one day. Randy and I did a lot and we saw a lot. We left an early wake-up call with the hotel, and were on our way to the train station by 11:00 a.m. Our train left at 1:40 p.m., and would get us home around 5 - 5:30 p.m. We both felt that this was an exceptionally good trip. Randy and I had scads of beautiful Easter flowers and plenty of accessories for a big Easter sale. The merchandise we bought would be delivered to the store within two weeks. We would be in great shape. I had planned on the girls decorating the store for Easter. Randy and I planned to put the huge tubs down the center of the store and each tub holding a different kind of flower. We could visualize how it would look but you wouldn't know until they were actually in place.

When the items Randy and I bought finally arrived within ten days of being purchased, we put the word out and we all began to decorate the store. The tubs in the center of the store were perfect for holding all the flowers we bought. We also bought several dozen vases - some ceramic and some imitation crystal. When the girls finished, the place looked like something out of a fairy tale. As you entered the store, you had to walk through and see everything on display. You had to do it. The store was that inviting. No one walked out of the store empty handed. Every customer bought something. We were doing a very brisk business. Women walked along the store, picking up some flowers as they went along. Then they found a vase that they liked, put the flowers in the vase, got a few more flowers and then checked out. I was happy as a lark.

The flowers and vases were my idea and I had earned my keep for a while longer. The candy was the first thing to sell out. Randy and I were both surprised at the way the candy sold. We did not reorder any candy; we were afraid it wouldn't move as the first order did. We had to reorder some small music boxes, baby toy chicks, bunnies and mechanical toys for the big kids (adults) along with other items that were good selling items. The store was busy until a few days after Easter. Big Ed was elated at the stores profit

margin. Randy and I both knew that it was better than Big
Ed had anticipated, and we weren't done yet. We planned on
having a big clearance sale to unload all the Christmas and
Easter merchandise that we had on hand and didn't sell
during either holiday. We planned on a Friday, Saturday and
Sunday clearance sale. Three days should move a lot of
merchandise. After store hours when Big Ed and the girls,
Gladys and Hazel, had gone for the day, Randy and I locked
the store and began getting sale items in the center of the
store in anticipation of the clearance sale. I found a big red
'Reduced Sale' tag which I affectionately stuck on Randy's
crotch. He looked at the tag and said,

"Never reduced for you sweetheart, for you…it's
free. Of course, you have to dig for it then it's yours." As I
walked by him, I gave him a playful pat on the ass and
hissed,

"Bitch." Of course, we both knew that this sort of
playfulness would lead to more serious folly… and it did.
We had great sex after we finished work. If only the walls
could talk.

Wednesdays were usually a dull day. We were never
that busy on Wednesdays, and if anyone wanted to do
something special, like keep a medical appointment, go
shopping, etc., Wednesday was the day to do it. Randy got a
call from Danny in the early afternoon, wanting to know if
we were going to be at the store for a while. Randy said yes,
we would be there until we closed the store. Danny said,

"Great, I'm coming up to see you and if Andy wants
to leave early, sit on him, hold him down until I get there."
Randy laughed and agreed to wait until Danny got there.
Randy couldn't tell me too much because he didn't know
anything. About 4:00 pm Big Ed left for the day, and the
girls were already gone. That left Randy and me in charge of
the store. Danny arrived a little later and was helping a very
handsome man in to our store. The man was dressed in
casual clothes, but had arm type crutches on both arms,
helping him drag his feet. Danny was helping him get in to

our store and seated in a chair. Once he was settled, Danny introduced Randy and me to Dave Hendricks, a marine sergeant recently assigned to the VA Hospital here in the Valley. Then the light bulb went on, and one and one made two. This was Andy's dream boat. He was indeed very handsome. So Randy called the barber shop and asked if Andy was busy. He wasn't. Then Randy asked him to run over to the store for a minute, which he did. When he flew in the store, as he always does, he saw Danny and said,

"What the hell are you doing here? Who's watching the bar?" Then a booming voice said,

"He brought me here so I could find you," said Dave. Andy, who didn't see the chair or anyone sitting there, moved toward the deep voice, saw Dave and screamed

"DAVE...IT'S YOU? OH MY GOD!! IT'S REALLY YOU?"

"None other, sweet thing," replied Dave. Well, their reunion was a happy event to see. They kissed each other and each shed a few tears; then, as a true Queen would do, Andy gave Dave hell for not writing for almost two years. Dave explained that he was injured and lost all his possessions including his wallet that had Andy's address in it. He was assigned to a field hospital for immediate attention. Then he was reassigned to San Diego for rehabilitation and had been there for about a year and a half. After pulling some strings, he got reassigned to the Maryland VA. All he could remember about Maryland was Uncle Mary's Club. When he could navigate, he took a cab to the club in an attempt to find you, talked to Danny, who remembered him; and here I am, thanks to Danny. Andy then began to talk about how he didn't know what to think since he hadn't heard from Dave. I thought I lost you overseas. Then he introduce Randy and me as brothers.

"These are two of my best straight friends and we work next door to each other. Del has been adopted by Randy's dad. I didn't know this until a couple of weeks ago.

"Randy", said Andy in all seriousness, "tell your father that I'm available for adoption, will you? I'm housebroken and don't require much. Honest, I'm serious." They all laughed and Dave said,

"If anyone is going to get you... it's me." Andy poked Dave on the arm and said,

"Oh, I love it when you act so butch." We all sat around and got better acquainted with Dave. He explained how he got shipped overseas and wound up in Pakistan. He was assigned to a group of fighters that went in ahead of the main body of soldiers, to case the place looking for arsenals and set off bombs, to blow them up before our troops got there. On his third assignment, he got wounded and both ankles were shattered. Then he was shipped to a field hospital that promptly sent him to a U.S. Hospital near Iran. From there, he was sent to San Diego for rehabilitation. He was there for about a year and a half and he learned he could request a transfer to a VA Hospital of his choosing. That's when he decided to come to Maryland VA Hospital if they could continue the rehabilitation program he was on. They had such a program and his transfer was approved. The rest is history. Since all his possessions were lost, he remembered the bar, Uncle Mary's, took a cab to the bar, remembered Danny and here I am. I plan to continue living at the VA and continue my therapy. Of course Andy has other plans. Andy reminded everyone that he lives just down the road from the VA. Embassy Arms is about two miles from the VA.

"Dave, you can move in with me, and take a cab to the VA for your therapy. When you're with me, I'll give you some therapy that you would never get from the VA." As I said, Andy had other plans for Dave. Again the crowd laughed at Andy.

"I might as well agree...," Dave smiling replied, "I won't have any peace if I don't." Andy was on cloud nine. Everything he ever wanted or talked about was coming true. He was so happy again; Dave was a very handsome marine.

Andy wanted us to go down to Uncle Mary's with him, Dave, and Danny, but we both politely refused. Randy and I had other things to do, and I felt that our needs were just as important as Andy's. We wondered if Dave's injuries could be corrected. Both ankles were shattered by a booby trap. The doctors were encouraging but it was going to take a long time. Randy and I were a bit doubtful. But Andy was going to play 'Nurse Nancy' and take care of Dave to the ultimate. Nothing was too good for her baby. We all knew that Dave would get expert treatment and loving care with Andy in charge.

Dr. Stiller had a call in for Randy and he wanted to talk to Randy privately. Randy made an appointment with him and was gone a whole afternoon. I was concerned for Randy. He didn't know what to expect and really was apprehensive about going to see the doctor, but he knew he wanted to and had to go. When he got back to the store, it was after 6 pm, the girls had gone home, and Big Ed and I were tending store. Randy was very selective in what he said about his visit to the doctor. He wanted to run some tests on him since he hadn't been to see the doctor in several years; strictly routine, nothing to worry about. Big Ed accepted Randy's explanation.

"It's been a long busy day guys. I think that I'll call it a day and head home. You mind?" We both said no, go home and get some rest and Big Ed left, saying

"If you're not busy, close early." When he was gone, I followed Randy into the office where I was met with a big pair of arms wrapped around me and he kissed me. There's a wonderful, indescribable feeling when a man hugs another man as I was being hugged. Randy whispered in my ear,

"I love you so much, I never want to lose you. You are my life and I can't see myself living without you. Don't ever leave me, please."

"Randy," I said, "I am not planning to leave you. I feel the same way. I can't picture myself living without you. I love you so much," and I began to smother him with kisses.

"What did the doctor have to say?"

"Well, Debbie has a severe problem. It's called bipolar disorder, and there's so many ways she could be affected by it. He feels that she is in the early stages and not a danger to herself or others."

"Danger? What danger and to who?" I asked.

"She could mame or kill herself, or someone in the family close to her." Randy went on to explain. "I explained her jealousy feelings about me and you to the doctor and he said this is one of the problems that loved ones in the family usually encounter. He said that this can be treated, and now is the time to start it before she gets any worse. The doctor also said that she is not aware of her problem, and he has got to figure out a way to help her without her knowing it.

"How can he give her medicine and not let her know what it's for?" I said to Randy.

"He's going to talk to a few of his colleagues for some professional help." And while Randy was telling me all of this, he still had me tightly in his arms and I began to embrace him. I could feel it. We were giving each other strength, much needed strength. Randy and I began kissing each other and I didn't want it to stop but we had to close the store, so we had to separate from each other and it was very hard for me to let him go. I didn't want this feeling to end, to leave me; I would have stayed like this all night with Randy and me in each other's arms. But we had the store to think of and all good things must come to an end. As we pulled away from each other, I saw a few tears in Randy's eyes, and of course that upset me and I shed a few tears too. Randy said,

"Don't worry, things are going to be just fine and remember, I love you very, very much." And we both left the office and began getting our work done.

CHAPTER 21 – A Shocking Phone Call

Time flies and marches on. Patti left yesterday for Canada with all four children. She would be gone for about three or four weeks with the Olympic ice team. Debbie planned on joining them in about two weeks. She claimed that she didn't want to miss her riding lessons and they were going to graduate in a few days. Patti didn't mind as long as Debbie would catch up with them in Canada. This left Randy and me together for a few weeks. The only thing we had to do was be sure the dogs were fed and walked. Not a problem. Randy did confide in me and say that Debbie was like a cat on a hot tin roof. So many little things irritated her. He was glad to leave the house and come to work just to get away from her. Graduation from the Riding Academy was on Saturday afternoon, April 13th and Debbie had planned to leave for Canada on Sunday, which would give her three full weeks with Patti and all the children.

Saturday afternoon, Randy had to go home and pick up some papers and prices for some merchandise he wanted to reorder from the Brooklyn show. He wasn't gone fifteen minutes, when I got a phone call from him to come to his house as soon as possible and tell no one where I was going. His voice sounded so strange that I got there as soon as I could. I walked in the kitchen door and saw Randy standing over the kitchen sink where he had vomited. I ran to his side and asked,

"Are you sick? What's wrong?" I gave him a glass of water which he refused. He motioned toward the dining room and when I walked in, I saw the bloody body of Debbie lying on the floor. On the dining room table was a big crystal and violet ashtray covered with blood. I took a good look at Debbie, felt her pulse, there was none, and saw blood on Randy hands and shirt.

"Randy" I cried, "What have you done?"

"I didn't do anything. I found her this way when I came in. I picked the ashtray up off her head, but she was dead," he sobbed. "Who would do this?"

"Have you called the police? "

"No, I called you. I don't know what to do." I hugged him as tightly as I could. I settled him in his living room on a recliner, and then called 911. I then called the store, talked to Big Ed and recommended he send the girls home, close the store, and get down to Randy's house as soon as possible. Big Ed got there about the same time as the police. The police came in, two detectives. One of them examined Debbie, pronounced her dead and phoned for the coroner. We were told not to touch anything. The detectives began to question Randy, over and over, until I was tired of hearing it. Big Ed called Syd Rosen his lawyer who said he's on his way. I was questioned as to the exact time Randy left the store. I replied to the best of my ability.

"Randy didn't kill his wife," I interjected.

"How do you know? You weren't here," barked one of the detectives. They bagged the ashtray and marked it as evidence. The coroner arrived with two more detectives and a few reporters arrived taking flash pictures. Syd arrived and threw out the reporters. Big Ed pulled the shades and caught hell from one of the detectives.

"I said don't touch anything and I mean ANYTHING." The coroner did a preliminary exam, bagged the hands and covered her with a sheet, waiting for the coroner to arrive and take the body to the morgue. A detective asked me,

"What's you're connection here? Who are you? Are you related to the victim?" Big Ed answered,

"They're both my sons and both were with me at the store when this happened. Neither one did this." Then a detective growled,

"We'll see." We were told not to leave the house and they began to question Randy relentlessly. Randy began to sob saying over and over,

"I didn't do this. I came home to get some papers from our last craft show and this is what I found. I loved her. Why would I do this?" I managed to move over closer to Randy and sat on the arm of the recliner. I put my arm around his neck but he was too upset to realize it was me. Syd stopped the rough questioning that Randy was being subjected to. He also reminded them that Randy has given them a statement and that unless they arrest him, they can stop the questioning and leave his home.

The police continued searching and questioning Randy, when Syd loudly told them to leave and let Randy alone. They all left except two detectives and they apologized for the roughness, but they had to get more information. Randy agreed to let them stay, but Syd said he was staying too, and as Randy's lawyer, he would be advising him. The questioning went on for about another hour when Syd said

"This interview is over. This man has suffered a severe shock and I'm sure he is totally confused. He lives here, has a business up the road about two blocks, he is not a flight risk. Let him have a good night's sleep...see him tomorrow."

The detective said to Randy, "We are going to have a detective here at the house all night. Can you sleep somewhere else tonight?"

I answered, "He can stay at my house, right next door. My wife and children are in Canada so the house is empty and will be for about two or three weeks." They left with a warning that none of us should leave town. The detective told Randy to get what he needed to take next door and leave his house, because he was going to lock all the doors and spend the night in the den. Big Ed hugged both of us and wanted to know if we wanted him to stay with us; if not he'd go home. Randy broke down and asked his dad to go home, get some sleep, and come back in the morning. When Big Ed left, Randy got some clean clothes, shaving gear and we went to my house where we were to spend many nights although we didn't know it at the time. With Randy in my bed, hugging me and me hugging him, he cried again, and I had to cry with him. Who would do this to Debbie? She had no enemies that we knew of.

We both cried ourselves to sleep, and I know I didn't sleep well at all during the night, and I know that Randy had a fitful sleep too. I got up early, showered and dressed for the day. I then went downstairs, made some coffee just as Randy came down, showered and dressed to join me. We both moved in total silence not knowing what to say. I didn't want him to break down again and I didn't want to cry again. I went on the porch to get the morning paper and when I went into the kitchen, I opened the paper, and said

"Those dirty fucking bastards." The headline read, "VALLEY SOCIALITE MURDERED, PLAYBOY HUSBAND PERSON OF INTEREST." And the byline gave her name, address and listed our names with Randy being the person of interest. Big Ed came in, cussing like a trooper. He too saw the paper and was fit to be tied. He had stopped next door and gave the detective a piece of his mind. We tried to explain that the police had nothing to do with it, it was the news reporters. He didn't give a damn, he had this on his mind and he had to unload. Big Ed had put a call in for Syd before he left his condo. The newspapers were blowing this out of proportion. Syd came to the house and told us all to try to go to work and not to answer any questions for anyone. Tell them it's under investigation and we were told not to discuss it. Randy couldn't work, nor could I. Not with an unsolved murder. Big Ed went to open the store and told the girls to run things until he got back. After about an hour or two, with police going over everything in the house, rooting for anything that would give them a clue. Big Ed went back to the store, explained as best he could to the girls what has happened and put a sign on the door that read, CLOSED TIL FURTHER NOTICE. He told the girls to go home until he called them back to work, and not to worry, they would be paid for time lost. Then he locked everything up and came back to the house. After several days, they came and arrested Randy for murdering his wife. His fingerprints were found on the ashtray. Randy had told the detectives that he picked up the ashtray from her body and placed it on the table. Randy then said,

"I live here. This is my home. You'll find my fingerprints all over this house." The police felt that this was sufficient to hold him on. Then the coroner's report showed that Debbie had been hit on the head several times with the heavy crystal ashtray, thus crushing her skull. She had hemorrhaged in her brain causing instant death. The report also showed that Debbie was two months pregnant.

"Impossible," cried Randy; "I had a vasectomy ten years ago. She couldn't have been pregnant." The detective in charge sarcastically replied,

"Maybe that's why you killed her, you found out that she was pregnant and you knew it wasn't yours. There's your motive." Big Ed and I both protested that the detective was wrong and Randy didn't kill his wife. The detectives took him out of my house in handcuffs and hauled him to the Valley Police Station where he was held without bail in a capital murder case. I contacted Patti in Canada and told her what happened. She broke down and cried. Big Ed wanted her to stay in Canada for a few more weeks so that the children wouldn't be exposed to all this publicity. He was sending her a check for several thousand dollars to cover her expenses with the children. She agreed and told me she didn't believe Randy did it either.

Alone in my room at night was the worst part of the day. I was so lonesome for Randy; I cried each night we were apart. I missed his strong arms around me, his smile, and his humor. I missed the little swat on the ass he would give me from time to time; or the wink he gave me when people were around and he couldn't do anything else. It's a horrible, horrible feeling. I wanted him back with me so badly that I was becoming irritable, with myself and with others. But everyone seemed to understand. After a few days of being separated, I began to have some doubts. Did he kill her? She knew something was going on but didn't know what. Did they have words that caused him to lose control and hit her? What if the police were right and Randy did kill her? I can't imagine living without Randy. Oh God, please make him be innocent - please.

My mind ran in many directions about this to the point that I felt I was losing it. I decided to open the store and go back to work. I called the girls and told them I was going to open the store next day. They were glad to come back to work. I went to visit Randy every day while he was in jail. It tore my heart apart to see him in jail, so helpless, so down hearted. Each time I saw him, I became more convinced than ever that he was innocent; and I, his best friend, was powerless to help him. I noticed that he was losing some weight too. Oh how I wanted to hold him, to kiss him and love him but only in my mind, not reality. After a few weeks, I began noticing bruises on his arms, small cuts on his face. He also had a slight limp. I asked him about them, he said they were nothing. Then one day when I visited him, he was limping more prominently than before. I asked him what happened, he said he fell and hurt his ankle. Another time I visited him, he had a black eye and swollen jaw. Again when I asked what happened, the guard answered and said,

"He fell down the stairs." Randy said nothing. I called Syd and told him what I had seen; Syd would pay a visit to Randy as his lawyer. Later that night, Syd came down to my house where Big Ed and I were having a drink. Syd said that even though Randy isn't talking, he feels that the police are beating him to get a confession. He said that a guard also told him that Randy fell down some stairs.

"That's a lot of bullshit. He didn't fall, those bastards beat him. He's on the first floor and the only thing in the basement are closed files, unsolved cases and office supplies. Randy is not permitted out of his cell, let alone to go down cellar stairs. He's in maximum security," Syd said. I'm making notes on all these things and when he is released, I'll file suit against them.

Time slowly moved on, too slowly for me, and Syd had quite a file against the police department. Randy always had another bruise or cut without an explanation. It broke my heart to be so near him and not be able to touch him. Oh God, how I wanted to touch him, to hold him. I wanted to beat up all the police that were responsible for Randy's bruises. In my mind, I did just that. I beat them all to a pulp, and they begged for mercy. In reality, nothing changed... I didn't want him to see me teary eyed or red eyes because he would know that I had been crying. Work at the store was a God send in a way.

I got involved with some sales and forgot what was going on around me. Many customers came in and expressed their sorrow for our loss and no one, no one believed that Randy harmed his wife. I got a phone call from Patti. She was home in the States and at our house with all four children. She had planned to stay a few more weeks, but the kids saw the news of the murder on Canadian TV, and they all wanted to come home so here we are. All the children would stay at our house, we had the room and Patti wouldn't have it any other way. Both dogs were there too. Patti agreed to try and shield the children as much as she could. Their classmates all knew what was going on and it would be hard to shelter them from everything. Andy and Dave came in and offered their help. What could they do? But the thought was there. Randy had been in jail for almost a month and the police were really hard on him. They were determined to get a confession, one way or another. We saw bruises and cuts along with black and blue marks but he never complained. I was outside in my back yard on a Sunday when the store was closed, playing with the two dogs. My heart was heavy because Randy was still in jail, and it looked like they were going to have a trial in a month and find him guilty.

My thoughts were broken by someone calling my name. It was Lenore Rodgers, my next door neighbor.

"Hi Lenore, I haven't seen you for quite some time. You been away?"

"Yes," she replied," we just got home last night and we heard the terrible news about Debbie. "How awful!"

"Yeah," I sighed, "Randy is being railroaded and we can't seem to stop it. Where were you? Did you have a nice trip?"

"Yes she replied, we had a three week cruise to Yugoslavia and then to Italy. Then we have some relatives in San Francisco so we stayed there for about five days. We got home last night. Poor Randy. I'd bet money he didn't harm his wife. When did it happen?" I answered that it was on March 13th. Lenore said,

"That's the day we left for our cruise. I was going over to tell Debbie that we would be gone for several weeks, but I heard some loud talking coming from her house and then our cab came so I never got to talk to her."

"Loud talking? Did you recognize the voice or see the person?"

"No, I was going over to her house when I heard the voices and our cab came and Wayne had to rush me into the cab so we would make our connections. I just heard them, not see them. Why? Is this important?"

"Yes," I almost shouted, "You may have heard the killer" "Oh my God", declared Lenore.

"You have to tell the police, Lenore. They need to know this."

"Yes, by all means," said Lenore. "I'll be glad to talk to them." A little later, Detective Patrick McCready asked Lenore to come over to my house where he began to question her. No, she did not see anyone, only heard their voices. Describe the voices.

"No it wasn't a man; it was two women talking loudly. I wanted to say good bye as we were leaving for several weeks and I wanted her to keep an eye on our house while we were gone. I never got to see her as our cab came and my husband has no patience. He rushed me into the cab. I had to leave without seeing her. Poor Debbie, I should have waited, maybe it would have saved her life." Lenore wiped away some tears. "I can't remember anything else."

Then the detective asked if she could remember anything out of the ordinary? Did you get a glimpse of the person arguing with Debbie? See a strange car? Lenore interrupted the detective,

"Wait a minute... I do remember seeing a car parked in the alley behind her house." Detective McCready perked up,

"What kind of car, what color, did you see a license number or part of it? Think hard, Mrs. Rogers, so much depends on your answers and your memory,"

"It was a red convertible. The license plate, I remember looking at it because it was so unusual. There is a lot of heavy shrubbery in the alley but I did get a look at the license plate. It had two horse heads on it, but I couldn't get a good look at the numbers on the plate because of the shrubs; I do remember the horse heads. I thought that the plate was unusual. That's really all I know, I didn't have much time with my husband rushing me towards the cab".

"Thank you Mrs. Rogers, you've been very helpful," said Detective McCready. He left with two policemen.

I received a call from Andy wanting to know if I was alright, could he do anything to help. Bless him; he might be gay, but his heart is in the right place. I told him no, there was nothing he could do at this time. There might be a break in the case. I briefed him on Mrs. Rogers.

"What was the name of the detective who interviewed your neighbor? I told him Patrick McCready. Andy moaned, "Oh God, you got BP."

"BP?" I repeated, "What's that mean?"

"In the gay world, he's known as BP, which stands for Big Prick. He is known for cruising around town where gay people hang out and pulling a gay guy into his car, takes him to a secluded spot and demands a blow job. If you refuse, he'll take you in and book you for soliciting. Most gays will give him a blow job. That's what they do and he does have a big cock, plus they don't want a police record. He's well known in the gay world, that bastard. Don't let on you know anything about him. What he doesn't know won't hurt him." I thanked him for the information, and said that I don't think I'll be having any conversation with him without my lawyer being present.

"You guys know that Dave and I love you both and will do anything we can to help. Just call us. I'll call you later to see how things going."

Syd arrived and I told him about Lenore and that Detective McCready questioned her. I brought him up to date on the convertible and told him I was looking for a miracle. Syd made a few phone calls from my house, jotted some notes, and then came back to Big Ed and me with the following information.

The red convertible is registered to Jake Trent, co-owner of Trent Farms and Valley Riding Academy. His designer license plate made the identity easy. I questioned the 'co-owner'. Syd said that his wife Gloria was also co-owner of the farms and the riding academy, but the convertible was registered to Jake Trent. Police were on their way to bring them both in for questioning. Syd said that he was going to the police station and wanted to be there when they were brought in and questioned; and for Big Ed and I to go to the store and he would keep us well informed if anything happens.

The rest of the day was the longest day I have ever had. Time crawled by and I was on pins and needles. Please God, let them send Randy home to us. We all know that he doesn't have a mean bone in his body. Please, please let him come home. I fought back some tears, but had to be careful in the store where we had customers. Big Ed was upset too but he didn't show it. He must have sensed my pain because he came over and put his arm around me and said,

"Don't worry Del, Randy will be fine. We both know that he didn't do this. He'll be fine." As I look up at Big Ed, I saw a tear or two in his eyes, and I said,

"I know you're right dad, but it's so hard to take right now." We hugged each other and went back to work. I should be consoling Big Ed and concerned about his heart condition and here he was consoling me. Big Ed was sad and happy; sad about Randy and happy that I called him 'dad'.

Syd was there when they brought in Gloria and Jake for questioning. Jake was in one room and Gloria in another. Jake's line of questioning was abruptly stopped when they learned that he was in Ocala, Florida on Friday morning, the day before the murder, and this was verified. He was there for two or three days. Jake was buying some horses for his farm and riding academy. He had an airtight alibi. They did ask for a DNA sample which he agreed to give.

"How many of your employees drive your red convertible when you're away?"

"None of them, well, my wife may drive it when she feels like it, although she has her own white Mustang." Gloria was to hold graduation classes for the Academy on Saturday the 13th, but cancelled the graduation due to the death of one of the students, Debbie. She claimed she was at the academy getting papers in order all day Saturday. When questioned about a red convertible being seen in the Bishop alley, she said it wasn't their car; it must be someone else's. Of course, Detective McCready wasn't satisfied with her answers to his questions so he kept hammering away. When he got tired, his assistant took over. She finally admitted that she was at the Bishop home, but that Debbie was alive when she left. They wanted to know why she was at her home. We had some business to discuss was the answer. This kept up for a few hours and when the police were not relenting, Gloria broke down crying and said that she and Debbie had an argument.

"Debbie and I settled our problem and I left. She was alive when I left." Detective McCready wanted more information, more details and he continued his line of questioning. Debbie did finally admit that their argument was over some money that Debbie owed the store for riding equipment.

"How much did she owe you and for what? Shot back Detective McCready. Gloria claimed that right off hand she didn't know, that she would have to get records from her office to answer his questions.

"Okay, we'll get the records and bring them here so you can explain what she owed you.

"Well, explained Gloria, it probably is merchandise that isn't logged in the ledger yet. I'll have to figure what it was and enter them. McCready was thinking ahead of Gloria and in a sarcastic tone asked Gloria,

"Look sweetheart, if you didn't know what she bought or how much she owed you ten minutes ago, how do you expect me to believe that you'll know when you have your ledgers here?"

Gloria began to show signs of becoming nervous and uneasy due to his line of questioning. McCready saw this and wouldn't stop his relentless line of questioning. He whispered to his assistant that she was getting nervous, look at her eyes, she should crack pretty soon. He began talking to her in a softer tone, however, to get her to open up to him. Gloria stuck to her original story, but added a few new details that were not mentioned before. Gloria added that in the heat of the argument, Debbie shoved her and she shoved back and when she did, Debbie fell, hitting her head on the edge of her table. When Debbie didn't move, I got scared and left.

"What was the argument about?" asked McCready, who didn't believe the money alibi.

"She was running around with my husband, and I wanted her to stop it."

"How did you know she was running around with your husband?"

"He was paying special attention to her as a student. He's done this before; she's not the first student that he has had sex with."

"Does your husband know that you are aware of his infidelities?"

"Yes, he does. He's no angel and he knows I know what he does."

"What time did you get there and what time did you leave?"

"I got there about 11 a.m. and left about 11:30 a.m."

"What were you wearing when you met with Mrs. Bishop?"

"I had on beige slacks and I think I had a brown pullover, yes I did," answered Gloria.

"Where are they now? At your home?" Inquired the detective.

"They are at my home, in my closet," replied Gloria.

The detective whispered to one of his assistants, who immediately left the house.

"And you're sure that no one else was in or around the house while you were there?"

"Not that I was aware of, no."

"You claim that she shoved you and you shoved her in return, and when you did, she hit her head on the edge of the table. Is that correct?"

"Yes it is - that's the way it happened."

"Well, there is no evidence that she ever hit her head on the table."

"Well she did and that's what happened."

"When we brought you and your husband down to the station today, you were both finger printed, and a swab of DNA was taken. Remember?"

"Yes, I do remember."

"Well, we found a finger print inside the ashtray of your right thumb. We found none of your husbands.'"

"Well, it's possible that I touched something while I was there."

"Your print was in dried blood."

"I can't explain that."

"OK ma'am" said Detective McCready,"its lunchtime and I'm sure you are hungry. I know I am. We'll break for lunch and be back here at 1:30 p.m. Officer Johnson will accompany you to lunch and will see to it that you are back here at 1:30 p.m." Officer Johnson came over, took Gloria by the arm and they left for lunch. McCready and several officers also left and they all met at the diner down the road for lunch. Gloria toyed with a sandwich but drank her coffee. Office Johnson ate her food but kept her eyes on Gloria. She obviously didn't trust her.

At 1:30 p.m., everyone was back at the house except Detective McCready, who met another detective and stopped to chat for a minute or two. He came in full of apologizes for being late, but no one seemed to care except him. The officer that was sent on an errand earlier in the day was back, reported to Detective McCready privately then left the room.

"Mrs. Trent," continued Detective McCready, "you said that the clothes you were wearing the day you met with Mrs. Bishop were in your closet. We checked your closet, your laundry room, in fact, we searched your house and could not find anything that you described. Are you sure of what you wore that day?"

"Yes I am," replied Gloria, "Your people must have over looked them."

"My people are very professional. They would not over look anything."

"No, I'm sure that they are there somewhere," replied Gloria nervously toying with her fingernails.

"Unless you got rid of the clothes, then they would not find anything," added McCready.

"I didn't get rid of anything," answered Gloria in a very weak voice.

"Why did you cancel the graduation services?"

"I felt that it wouldn't be right to have a happy celebration service after a student had died."

"We have talked to your staff and trainers at the academy. They said that you cancelled the service around 12 noon."

"Yes, I did. Who could conduct a happy service as our graduation would be, when you have had a tragedy occur to one of the graduates."

"Well, Mrs. Trent, why did you cancel the service at around noon using the death of your student as your excuse, when the coroner and Police Department didn't make a formal statement and release that information to the press until after 3 p.m.?"

"There must be some mistake. I'm sure that I heard somewhere that she had been killed."

"Not so," replied the detective. The news was released by the coroner at 3:00 p.m. You told your staff at noon. To which she replied

"I can't explain it," and she began to sob again.

"Were you aware that Mrs. Bishop was two months pregnant?"

"I knew she was pregnant but didn't know it was two months," she continued sobbing softly.

"Did her pregnancy come up in your conversation with her?"

"Yes, it did. She wanted Jake to pay for her abortion and I told her that I wasn't using my money to pay for her playing around."

"Is that when she shoved you?"

"She didn't shove me, she slapped my face."

"Then what happened?"

"I slapped her back."

"You didn't shove her?"

"No, I slapped her." Then Gloria broke down again and began crying almost hysterical. "I didn't want to kill her; I wanted her to leave my husband alone."

Then the detective said in a very soft voice,

"Is that when you picked up the ashtray and hit her with it?"

Gloria answered, barely auditable, "Yes, but I never intended to kill her." Then they brought her husband in and when Gloria saw him, she exploded,

"And you, you rotten son of a bitch" she jumped up out of her chair to strike him and had to be restrained by the detective and a policeman. Jake jumped behind a policeman to avoid getting hit by his wife. "You never could keep it in your pants. If you couldn't fuck every girl you saw, you felt cheated somewhere. I hope you rot in hell for the misery you've put me through you slimy bastard. I know all about the women you've been fucking at the Academy. How dumb do you think I am?"

Syd left this questioning and went before a sitting judge and demanded the immediate release of Randolph Thomas Bishop based on the confession of Mrs. Gloria Trent. The judge instructed his staff member to verify if this was true. Did they have a confession? If they did, then bring Mr. Bishop before him. As Randy was brought before the judge, the judge said,

"Mr. Bishop, I have reviewed the happenings of your case and must first extend to you the profound sorrow of this court and myself, on behalf of the loss of your wife. Secondly, I must apologize to you for myself and the State of Maryland for any injustice you may have suffered while incarcerated for a crime you didn't commit. I see you have your lawyer present. Sir, you are free to go.

Syd then told me that he was going to my house and to bring Randy there. He would have a photographer there to take pictures of Randy's cuts and bruises for his lawsuits. Syd wasted no time; he was on his cell phone to his offices, instructing his staff to prepare the necessary papers to file a lawsuit against The Trent Farms and another against the Valley Riding Academy for wrongful death and false imprisonment; as well as The Hamilton Valley Police Department and the State of Maryland both for police brutality. Syd was going to pick up Big Ed on his way.

"See you at the house."

When Randy finally came out of the police station, he looked so drawn and weary and oh so tired, and he was limping. It was pouring down rain. My poor baby. We didn't have an umbrella but who cares. I took him in my arms and said,

"Sweet Mother of God! What have they done to you?" He turned his face away from me so that that I couldn't see it. I placed my hands behind his neck and ears and firmly held his face so that I could see what his face looked like. His lip was swollen, he had a butterfly patch over his right eye, and his left jaw was black and blue. With the rain running down our faces, no one could see that we were both crying. Randy tried to hide his face and said,

"Don't look at me, I feel so ashamed."

"Look Randy, I love you more now than ever, don't ever, ever be ashamed with me.

"They tried their damnedest to get me to confess but I would never confess to something I didn't do." I put my arms around him and gave him a kiss, a kiss that I wanted to give him weeks ago, and couldn't. I gave him several kisses.

"Del, we're being watched, all the cops..." warned Randy. I looked towards the police station and saw several policeman watching us. I hugged him tighter, positioned his face in my hands, and looked at the watching police. I kissed his eye, his jaw and kissed him passionately on his lips, which were quivering, again. I did this for all the policemen to see and I said,

"Let the bastards look, who gives a good fuck?" I kissed him again and again and said, "Let's go home!" We limped, due to Randy's bad leg, out of the police parking lot and headed down the street, in the pouring rain, to my car, headed for home.

CHAPTER 22 - A Welcome Home

With heavy rain coming down on us, Randy and I got into my car, and we drove home. I helped Randy into my kitchen when the door opened, his children and mine shouted,

"Dad, Uncle Randy", as they ran to kiss and hug him. Even the dogs were barking, as he was sorely missed. Patti embraced him and gave him several kisses and then his father finally got to hug and kiss his son, saying,

"We have all missed you and are so thankful to God that you are home with us again. We all knew that you were innocent of this terrible crime." There wasn't a dry eye in the house at this reunion. Syd waited until last to say,

"Welcome home Randy. You're a free man now, you didn't deserve the treatment they gave you, but they will pay for what they have done and how they've treated you." Even Syd had to wipe a tear or two from his eyes. "I have a photographer here to take pictures of your entire body, showing the bruises that you received while in jail. After the pictures are taken, take a shower, get into some comfortable clothes and enjoy your family."

Syd Rosen, the family lawyer for the Bishop's, filed three lawsuits: one against the Hamilton Valley Police Department for police brutality; one against the State of Maryland for failure to control Hamilton Valley Police Department; and one against Gloria Trent for the murder of Debbie Bishop. Randolph Thomas Bishop collected on all three lawsuits.

Syd Rosen, a family friend and lawyer for the Bishop's for many, many years, handled all cases Pro Bono.

The End